TOM SWIFT®
TERROR ON THE MOONS OF JUPITER
VICTOR APPLETON

WANDERER BOOKS
Published by Simon & Schuster, New York

Copyright© 1981 by Stratemeyer Syndicate
All rights reserved
including the right of reproduction
in whole or in part in any form
Published by WANDERER BOOKS
A Simon & Schuster Division of
Gulf & Western Corporation
Simon & Schuster Building
1230 Avenue of the Americas
New York, New York 10020
Manufactured in the United States of America
10 9 8 7 6 5 4 3
WANDERER and colophon are trademarks
of Simon & Schuster
TOM SWIFT is a trademark of Stratemeyer Syndicate, registered in
the United States Patent and Trademark Office
Library of Congress Cataloging in Publication Data
Appleton, Victor, pseud.
Terror on the moons of Jupiter.
(His Tom Swift; 2)
SUMMARY: Tom Swift and his friends Ben and Anita travel
with their new robot, Aristotle, to the moons of Jupiter where
they encounter a sinister rival.
[1. Science fiction. 2. Robots—Fiction]
I. Title.
PZ7.A652Te   [Fic]   80-26446
ISBN 0-671-41182-9
ISBN 0-671-41183-7 (pbk.)

CONTENTS

Chapter One

"Hit the deck!" Tom Swift yelled, tucking his six-foot frame into a compact ball and rolling backward. He came out of the roll in a balanced crouch and stared in horror. The massive, metal arm of his robot whizzed past him, exactly where his rib cage had been only seconds before.

Ben Walking Eagle and Anita Thorwald reacted instantly to Tom's warning. They fell straight to the floor, cushioning the impact with the palms of their hands.

It was just in time. The robot's multi-jointed arm ripped through the heavy steel bulkhead. Then it stopped, its naked struts and wires caught in the jagged edges of the hole it had just torn in the lab of the spaceship *Daniel Boone.*

Alarms began to clang throughout that section of the giant craft.

"Stop program!" Tom shouted at the squat mechanoid. "Shut down for reprograming."

There was a whirring sound and then Tom, Ben, and Anita heard the squish of traction pads on the deck. The robot's mainframe and motor-frame rotated ninety degrees, then jerked to a halt. All of its sections now faced forward, except for the pinned arm.

"At least the EXCOM circuit is working," Anita remarked dryly. The supple redhead stood up and brushed vigorously at the now dirty knees of her white jumpsuit. Tom winced at her remark as he moved to shut off the alarm.

The robot's EXCOM—or EXterior COMmunications circuit—translated human speech into binary numbers by using pitch, rather than actual consonant and vowel sounds, as references. EXCOM made vocal command possible by exactly identifying human vocal frequencies and translating them in terms of cycles per second.

There was the sound of running feet in the corridor outside and the door was thrown open by a security guard.

"What's going on here?" the guard sternly demanded.

Tom threw the switch which silenced the shrill clanging. "Everything is under control, Officer," he said. In the sudden quiet his voice sounded loud. "I apologize for the disturbance. The robot malfunctioned rather suddenly, causing a bit of damage before it could be stopped. Nobody was hurt."

The security officer scowled at the robot, whose arm was still in the bulkhead, then at Ben who was slowly getting up from the floor. Behind the officer the members of the Security Alert Emergency Team crowded around the entrance to the lab.

"This sort of 'disturbance' as you call it is a very serious matter—especially on a spaceship streaking through space to Jupiter," the officer insisted sternly. "The *Daniel Boone* cannot afford carelessness like this. What if the lab was not deep inside the ship? What if this thing—" he gestured to the metallic robot—"had tried to punch a hole in the outside bulkhead? Do you have any idea how serious that would have been, young man?" He was glaring at Tom.

"Now hold on a minute!" Ben exclaimed angrily. "Do you know who you are talking to? That just happens to be Tom Swift, the person whose inventions and hard work made this spaceship possible in the first place."

Indeed, Benjamin Franklin Walking Eagle had met the young inventor while Tom was developing his Prometheus drive which now was powering the *Daniel Boone* through space at speeds faster than man had ever gone. Tom and his tall, dark-haired, Cherokee Indian friend had first successfully tested the revolutionary new drive in their speedy ship, the *Davey Cricket,* beating Anita Thorwald in a recent space race. Now the three friends were afraid they were in trouble.

"Ben, the officer is right," Tom said mildly. He knew his robot was not strong enough to damage the outside hull of the spaceship, but this accident had scared him more than he wanted to admit. A spaceship deep in outer space was certainly no place for accidents of any kind. If Ben or Anita—or even he, Tom—had been hurt badly, emergency medical treatment would have been limited to what was available on the *Daniel Boone.* True, the ship's medical facilities were the best possible, under the circumstances, but it still was not like having an entire hospital Earthside.

"I take full responsibility for the accident," Tom told the officer. "As you can see for yourself the damage—fortunately—is not great. My friends and I will put things in order."

With a dubious look still on his face, the security officer and his men left the lab.

"You might at least have let them stay and help clean up this mess," Anita protested. "Or do you think I'll do most of the picking up since I'm a girl?"

Tom did not hear her. He was already deep in thought, gazing up at the robot's "face." At the moment, the sensorframe was incomplete and only the sonar transducers, the robot's sole means of "seeing," were in place. By emitting ultrasonic beams in all directions and "listening" for echoes, the mechanoid could sense its direction from objects and thus avoid bumping into things. Ultimately, it would have other kinds of sight as well. Television cameras and photosensitive arrays would be part of its sensor system, allowing it to see in several ways, depending on the conditions. Sonarscan, however, would always have the advantage of requiring the least amount of power.

"Poor, dumb, half-blind machine," Tom said out loud.

"You talk as if you actually feel sorry for it," Ben said. He walked over to the young inventor and put a consoling hand on Tom's shoulder. Ben's vast knowledge of computers and his great talent for programing them had been invaluable in making the robot.

"I do feel sorry for it," Tom said.

"Ah, Herr Doctor Frankenstein," quipped Anita, "you have created a monster!"

Ben patted the metal shoulder of the robot protectively. "Shh! You'll hurt its feelings!"

"I forgot that it's still 'on'! Can it hear what we're saying?" Anita asked.

"I doubt it," said Tom, "although when I gave it the 'shut down for reprograming' instruction, it only locked its servodrive in the forward position."

He rummaged through his toolbox and withdrew something resembling a screwdriver with a pointed tip. It had a black wire coming out of the handle with an alligator clip on the end. In the handle was a place for a digital readout.

The young inventor peered into the mass of interwoven wires and hydraulic lines in the robot's shoulder and, a moment later, carefully selected a red wire. He clipped the tool's "pigtail" onto the robot's mainframe, and then stabbed through the red wire's insulation with the pointed end. He watched the digital readout for a moment, then nodded in satisfaction.

"Now that the robot's nuclear cells are operational, it can't be totally shut down except by special equipment," he said. "I've got continuity, so the arm is intact."

Anita looked at the mechanoid uncertainly.

Outwardly, it remained motionless and silent, its only sign of life a tiny, glowing light on the sensorframe. Her gaze fell on the injured arm. "Uh-oh! We've got a problem, Tom," she said, bending closer to the robot's wrist. "Look at this!"

Anita pointed to the ripped bulkhead and Tom groaned as he watched a small drop of oily fluid dribble down the smooth metal surface.

"The metal of the bulkhead must have cut through a hydraulic line," he said. "It's a good thing you noticed that fluid, Anita, because that line would never have held pressure. We'd have had a real mess on our hands if that stuff had started squirting out under load!"

For all its electronic complexity, the robot was a very simple mechanism in many ways. For sheer operating efficiency, power, and speed of response, Tom had chosen to go with electrohydraulics, a basic power system that functioned on the principle that oil in a confined space cannot be compressed. When pressure is applied to any part of it, that pressure is transferred throughout the oil with no loss of energy.

The robot had electrically activated hydraulic cylinders at all of its movement points. An electronic signal, given by the central processing unit for a specific movement, activated a piston inside a particular cylinder. The piston put pressure on the hydraulic fluid—the oil—and that pressure was transferred throughout the line. The robot's movement was limited only by the receptiveness of the pressure sensors, which Tom had worked very hard to make as sensitive as possible.

"There's a pinhole rupture in the green line," Tom said, peering closely at the damaged arm. "We'll have to heatseal it so that the line will hold pressure until we can replace it."

"I'll do it," said Ben. The young computer technician went to a metal cabinet and returned with a tool that looked like a futuristic ray gun, but was actually a small laser. Ben held a tiny piece of patching plastic with a pair of forceps and heated it with the laser. Then he placed the hot plastic over the pinhole and held the laser beam on it for a few seconds until it fused with the hydraulic line.

"We'd better get to work and untangle that arm now," said Anita. "The robot must be pretty bored standing there like that!"

For the next two hours, Tom, Ben, and Anita painstakingly untangled the robot's arm from the mass of broken wires and jagged metal of the bulkhead.

"It makes you appreciate the complexity of the

human body," Ben remarked as they worked carefully. He extracted a wire from the robot's wrist with a pair of long, thin tweezers. "Until we started working on this thing, I never realized how complicated even a simple movement, like picking up a glass of water, is. It probably takes billions of nerve impulses from the brain just to hold a glass without dropping it! You're a wiring genius, Tom Swift!"

Tom smiled modestly and protested, "All three of us built this robot. You and Anita worked just as hard as I did." He extracted the last broken wire from the mechanoid's arm. "Until we know what went wrong with the robot, I don't think we should give it any complicated instructions," he cautioned. "The trouble is, I can't move that arm. In fact, I doubt the three of us can move the robot."

Anita and Ben nodded in silent agreement. The rip in the bulkhead spoke for itself. The robot was just too heavy to be pushed around like a piece of furniture.

Tom had known from the beginning that weight and maneuverability would be as important to the design of his robot as its brain. He also knew that it would have to withstand and survive the worst conditions man and machine had ever faced. A balance had to be achieved without sacrificing either durability or efficiency.

Only part of the problem had been solved on Earth at the main complex of Swift Enterprises in Shopton, New Mexico. Tom had used the company's giant Langley computer to formulate a new, lightweight steel and had incorporated as much of it as possible in the construction of the mechanical man. But the robot still weighed a lot! It took miles of wiring, 300 pounds of steel, and a sensorframe of almost two hundred pounds to duplicate only some human functions with a third of the efficiency!

Tom's expression brightened suddenly. "I've just thought of something! If Anita doesn't mind, we can use her computer to bypass the robot's central programing unit!"

Ben nodded thoughtfully. "You mean, use her computer as the robot's brain," he asked, "so we can get it to move itself to the big computer terminal over in the engineering section?"

"Exactly. Once it's there we can do a circuit check and run the complete program to see what made the robot suddenly go berserk."

He turned and looked at the beautiful redhead. Several years before, Anita's right leg had been crushed in an accident. Unable to save the leg, doctors had replaced it with an artificial limb which in many ways was superior to her natural leg. Among other features, the artificial leg housed a computer.

Tom did not want Anita to think she was being forced to volunteer for anything she did not want to do. He knew how sensitive she was, at times, about having lost her real leg and besides, he had been on the receiving end of her temper on more than one occasion and had no wish to ever repeat the experience if he could help it!

To his relief, Anita smiled and rolled up her jumpsuit, exposing the computer. All circuits were visible through the clear plastic outer covering. Shaped to resemble a human leg, it was made of a thin layer of clear gel sandwiched between two pieces of pliable, high-density plastic.

Anita's link with the computer was a large bracelet on her right wrist. It contained a microterminal with a LED crystal face and a surrounding display of buttons in various colors. The wrist controller was connected by a microscopically thin wire that went through Anita's arm, down her side, and through the main artery in her right leg to the computer.

The young woman held her wrist out. "Glad to help. Which one of you is going to do the honors? I'm afraid this idea is a bit beyond my programing capabilities."

"Why don't you take care of that, Ben, while I do the wiring?" said Tom. "I want to do this with a series hookup instead of by radio. That way, nothing can go wrong."

Ben sat down next to Anita and gently took her wrist. "What should we call this program?" he asked.

"How about 'a program to move the robot,' and getting on with it," Anita said impatiently.

"You have no sense of humor," complained Ben. Nevertheless he began punching buttons on the wrist controller, humming softly to himself.

It took almost an hour but at last everything was ready.

"The robot won't be able to boogie, but it will move—as long as Anita's computer is in control," said Ben.

"You and your robot friend make a beautiful couple, Anita," Tom teased. "Have you set the wedding date yet?" He barely had enough time to duck as the volatile redhead swung at him with her left hand, growling, "Watch it, buster!" She was standing next to the silent robot, connected to it by a heavy-gauge, four-foot-long adapter cable that Tom had rigged to go from her wrist controller to the robot's sensorframe.

"We'll have to take it *very* slowly because we don't have EXCOM," said Tom. "Luckily, there aren't a lot of turns to make, once we get out of the lab. The turns will be the hardest maneuvers. Is everybody ready?"

Ben and Anita nodded. Tom walked across the room to the hatch and pressed the control. The pneumatic door hissed softly and opened. "Activate him," said Tom. He watched tensely as Ben punched out the signal on Anita's wrist controller.

There was a sharp, loud, popping sound, then an electric crackle. The robot jerked spasmodically from its wrist to a nearby dangling bulkhead wire. The insulation on the wire bubbled for a moment.

The robot jerked again. This time, Anita screamed as the current arced from the robot's arm to the bulkhead wire!

Chapter Two

"Abort!" yelled Tom, as Ben grabbed for Anita's wrist controller.

Once again the clang of the alarms shattered the silence of that section of the spaceship.

Suddenly, a thin stream of hydraulic fluid shot out from the robot's wrist and splashed on the bulkhead.

"It's from the blue line," Ben shouted. "I didn't see any fluid leaking from that one!"

Another spark shot from the robot's wrist to the bulkhead and the hydraulic fluid exploded into flame. Ben was driven back by the sudden heat of the fire and Anita fell to her knees!

20 The high-pitched whine of the fire alarm now

joined the ongoing clang of the general alarm.

The room was filling rapidly with thick, blue-green smoke as the hydraulic fluid fed the electrical fire. Tom was barely able to see Anita as he rushed to her side. She was obviously frightened but still in control of herself. He reached for her wrist controller, but the young woman wrenched her arm away.

"There's no time for that," she yelled. Wrapping the adapter cord around her fist, she jerked it as hard as she could.

"No," yelled Tom, "don't do that!" He tried to get the cord out of her hands, but Anita seemed to possess superhuman strength. A tongue of flame shot out of the bulkhead as the insulation on the electrical wires fed the fire. Tom put his arm across his eyes to protect them from the severe heat and he caught a brief glimpse of Anita using the massive robot as a shield.

Ben coughed from somewhere in the room, but the thick, toxic smoke prevented Tom from seeing if his friend was hurt.

Tom staggered dizzily back to Anita's side and grabbed for her wrist again. This time, however, he was off balance and the redhead gave him a mighty shove that sent him to the deck.

What happened next seemed to Tom like a slow-motion, haze-enveloped, nightmare ballet.

He saw Anita brace her natural leg against the robot and pull the adapter cord with all her strength. The cord stretched, then popped free of the rubber connector boot. The robot jerked once more and was still.

The adapter cable was still wrapped around Anita's hands. Tom noticed sparks coming from the filaments on the broken ends as she staggered backward, away from the robot. But something was wrong with her, Tom's smoke-fogged eyes told him. She looked like a rag doll that had been tossed out of a window. He opened his mouth to call to her, but choked as the thick, hot smoke poured down his throat. Then he saw her fall, face down, to the deck.

Where were the emergency squads? Tom wondered. The two different alarms continued to sound in the hallway, yet the usually prompt rescue teams had not responded.

Tom knew if he did not get air soon, he would collapse, and he and his two friends would die. He heard Ben gasping for air just as he was doing. As for Anita, she was lying motionless on the floor. Tom could only hope she was not badly injured.

Air! He needed air and the fire was taking it all.

Tom put his face down against the deck and

took shallow breaths. As long as he had air, he could stay conscious—and live! As long as the fire had air, it would continue to burn. How could he cut off air to the fire?

"First I must get Ben and Anita out," Tom gasped out loud.

"Ben!" he yelled. His throat felt raw from the heat and smoke and his yell was more of a gurgle than anything else.

The answer was a deep coughing to his left.

Tom stayed as low to the deck as he could. Slowly, he crawled in Ben's direction. It seemed to take a long time just to move a foot or two. "Left hand out, pull. Right hand out, pull," Tom instructed himself.

The outline of Ben's body finally appeared through the smoke. The young Indian was struggling to rise.

"Easy, Ben," Tom said. He grasped his friend's shoulder and shook it, weakly.

"Tom—"

"We have to get Anita out! I need your help!"

"How—"

"Follow me."

Everything seemed to be taking a long time, but Tom knew that not more than four or five minutes could have passed since that first explosion. Still, that was considerably more than the emergency squads had ever needed to respond to an alarm during their practice drills. Where was the team which had been to the lab only moments before?

They crawled toward a splotch of bright light that flickered hazily through the thick smoke. Anita should be there, Tom thought.

She was. Both boys could feel their strength leaving them. There wasn't much time left. The fire was spreading rapidly to the lab furniture. Soon it would find new fuel inside the cupboards and on the shelves of the work area.

As carefully as he could, Tom grasped Anita's arm near the shoulder with one hand. With the other he took a firm hold on her jumpsuit near the waist. Ben did the same.

They pulled the unconscious girl, then stopped, choking and gasping for air. The process was agonizingly slow, but somehow, an eternity later, they were through the lab door and into the corridor.

Just then Ben fainted. Tom was close to doing the same when, through the fog of semiconsciousness, he became aware of the sound of footsteps.

A second later, he heard muffled voices shouting words that were vaguely recognizable, and he felt strong hands grab hold of him.

The robot! He had forgotten all about it. He struggled to break free of the hands. He tried to explain about the robot, but his rescuers were not paying any attention.

With the last of his strength, Tom wrenched free and lurched against the lab door.

". . . Seal off . . . robot. . ." he managed to croak.

He felt the press of bodies against him. Then the door began to close. Someone shoved an oxygen mask over his face. At first it threatened to smother him, but he gasped, and involuntarily inhaled the life-giving air. He took more breaths, greedily gulping it in, until his head began to clear. He was aware of more than just hands now, and saw the eyes of the emergency crew through their oxygen masks.

"Evacuate the chamber!" Tom shouted. The words sounded alien and distorted through his mask. The emergency squad seemed confused, and nobody moved.

Quickly, Tom reached for a small door fitted into the bulkhead and jerked it open. Reaching in, he grasped a large red handle. But he did not pull it down immediately. Tendrils of the thick smoke were curling out from the edges of the lab door. It was not closed all the way!

"Help me seal the chamber," Tom said. He

put all his weight against the heavy steel door and heard the hinges whine. Two members of the crew followed his example and a third spun the locking wheel. Then Tom reached for the handle and pulled it all the way down.

A nearby compressor chugged to life. The fire would be out within minutes as all the air was sucked from the sealed lab. That was one of the safety features of the *Daniel Boone*. A vacuum could be created in any part of the giant ship, and all chambers could be sealed off from one another.

Tom sagged against the door, exhausted. He examined himself for the first time and saw that his clothing was torn and sooty. His hands were stung and blisters began to appear on them. He felt the last bit of energy drain from his body as he stared at the emergency crew.

They seemed detached and alien-looking. With their dark masks, only their eyes were visible. Tom blinked. Five human beings with grotesque elephant snouts.

He laughed to himself. It was comical.

His knees buckled and he let himself fall. The release felt good.

Gratefully he sank into darkness.

Chapter Three

"Dad?"

"Welcome back to the world, Son."

Tom's eyes fluttered open. It was amazing how he had sensed his father, even before seeing him. It was like being in the presence of a . . . *presence.* But then, his father had that effect on many people. His character had been forged by years of hard work. His many famous inventions had benefited people throughout the world as well as the pioneers in space. Often his explorations had endangered his life, but his quick thinking and ingenuity had always saved the day. The elder Swift's creative genius and dynamic force of will still urged him to even greater exploits.

27

He looked fondly down at his son who was so much like him in so many different ways.

Tom's vision came into focus and he saw that he was in the ship's infirmary.

"We wanted to make sure you had no internal injuries," his father said. "Doctor Ling has given you his seal of approval!"

"How long have I been here?" The memory of the fire suddenly flooded back to Tom. With a tingling shot of adrenaline, it brought him totally awake.

"About a day," replied his father.

"What about Anita?" Tom asked anxiously.

"Doctor Ling is with her. She's fine, but she's in Intensive Care because there is no more room here."

"And Ben?"

"Did someone mention my name?"

Tom heard the metallic swish of a hospital privacy curtain, and he rolled over to see his friend lying on a bed next to his.

The young Indian smiled mischievously. "Except for those fancy pink hands, you look okay!"

Tom remembered his burns and held up his hands. They had indeed been sprayed with *Medicote,* an antibiotic preparation that left a protective film, like a new skin, over a wound. It kept dirt out, but let air in for healing. It would disappear in time. Tom had once asked a doctor why *Medi-cote* was pink. The man had looked at him as though he had missed the obvious. "Why, so we know it's *there,* of course!"

"How long do I have to stay here?" Tom asked his father.

"You can leave any time you want, but if I were you, I'd put on some clothes first."

Tom blushed and looked at the hospital gown he was wearing.

The elder Swift smiled. "You'll find some things in the closet. After you get dressed, meet me outside. The captain wants to see us."

"Has he been down to the lab?" Tom asked.

"I don't know. It's not what he wants to talk to us about."

"Dad—" The young man got out of bed. Every muscle in his body protested the act.

Mr. Swift turned from the infirmary hatch and looked at his son. "I know," he said gently. "It was an accident. You did the best you could. I'm just glad you are all right."

"What took the emergency squad so long to respond to the alarms?" Tom asked.

"There was a malfunction in the central security switchboard," his father explained. "The squad was sent to an area on the other side of the ship."

Tom looked puzzled. "But a team had just responded to the first alarm. They barely had time to get back to their base before the fire."

"Didn't anyone even hear the alarms?" asked Ben. "Those things are loud. I thought they'd be heard all the way to Jupiter!"

Tom's father nodded slowly. "It was someone passing through a neighboring corridor who turned in the alarm. The first team had returned to Security Base Two so they were out of your area. It just happened that you three were the only people in the lab area at that time. Everyone else had either finished for the day or taken their dinner break." Mr. Swift paused, then added, "The main alarm system, as well as its backup, will be checked daily from now on."

He looked gravely at the two boys. "We were all most fortunate this time. We can't count on that kind of luck again." Then he turned, ducked slightly to clear the top of the hatch, and left the infirmary.

After getting dressed, Tom met his father at the ship's main elevator. "Bridge," the elder Swift said into the control speaker.

"Thank you," said a machine voice. There was a sensation of movement. The elevator was controlled by the ship's computer and the voice activation worked on the same principle as the EXCOM circuit in Tom's robot.

"Any news from the Argus probe?" Tom asked.

"No, we're getting the usual crazy signals. The thing has been no good at all since it landed on Io. The radiation must have gotten to it."

Io was the innermost of the Galilean moons of Jupiter. In 1610, the great scientist and astronomer, Galileo, discovered Io and her three sister moons, Callisto, Europa, and Ganymede, and named them after characters in the myths about Zeus, king of the Olympian gods, who was also known as Jupiter. They were Jupiter's largest moons and the ones of foremost interest to scientists.

The probe, which Tom had named Argus after the mythical giant with a hundred eyes, had been designed and built by Swift Enterprises. Its "hundred eyes" were supposed to scan the Galilean moons.

The probe had functioned perfectly throughout the first part of its mission, but after landing on Io, its signals had suddenly become so distorted that no one could make any sense out of the data.

"Bridge," the computer announced. The

doors of the elevator slid open and Tom and his father walked out into the brain center of the *Daniel Boone*. A short distance away, the captain, wearing a U. S. Navy jumpsuit, stood waiting for them, leaning casually on a bulkhead support.

"Rafe," Mr. Swift said with a smile and held out his hand. "How is it going?"

"Fine, Tom, just fine." The captain was a full four inches shorter than either Tom or his father, but heavier in build.

"Captain Barrot," Tom said, more formally. As far as he knew, his father was the only man on board ever permitted to call the captain by his first name.

Until the *Daniel Boone* project, Captain Rafe Barrot had been one of Swift Enterprises's senior-grade freighter pilots—the youngest in the company's history. During the construction of the ship, the daring pilot was drafted to help ferry supplies and materials to the work site from Earth and from the *New America* space colony.

Swift Enterprises was the chief contractor on the *Daniel Boone*, but it was a government project, and all during the construction phase there had been controversy over how the giant ship would be outfitted and staffed. All branches of the military wanted the contract and the bidding was lively. That is how Rafe Barrot got the job.

"The navy needs you, Son," he was told by Admiral Harris. Barrot loved to repeat this story and he did a fair imitation of the crusty admiral's voice. "For forty years, I've had to sit and watch those air force boys get all the glory for the space program while the navy got the 'privilege' of fishing for the capsules. No more! We've got to grow or die, and I say we should be up there! Space is the ocean of the universe and that's the navy's territory!"

No one had taken the old admiral seriously, until it was disclosed that the navy's bid was the lowest, so it had won the contract.

Because of Rafe Barrot's background in the naval air force and his experience as a space pilot on large vessels, he was called back into service, restored to the rank of captain, and given command of the *Daniel Boone*.

The years as a civilian had left their imprint on him, however. Tom was aware of how sharply Barrot's relaxed manner contrasted with that of his crew of career navy men. It did not mean that the captain took his job less seriously than they did, it was just his way.

Now Rafe Barrot smiled his usual friendly smile and motioned for the two Swifts to follow him. "We've decided on a location for the Ganymede base," he said. "Come to the chartroom with me. I'd like to hear your feedback."

Tom recognized that this invitation was a courtesy extended only to him and his father because of their long-standing friendship, rather than duty. Even though Swift Enterprises had built the *Daniel Boone,* the Swifts were civilian members of the scientific staff of the expedition. They had no authority in matters pertaining to the running of the ship. In fact, few civilians were ever permitted on the bridge and, by the same token, few of the navy crew were ever seen in the sections assigned to the scientists and other civilian personnel.

The chartroom of the *Daniel Boone* bore little resemblance to a traditional, ocean-going ship's chartroom, where the captain of the vessel went to plot a course. There were no charts here, only a computer terminal and a giant wall screen.

Captain Barrot sat down at the terminal and punched out a code. The wall screen was suddenly filled with the harsh terrain of Ganymede, third moon out from Jupiter's surface and the largest of the planet's major moons.

"What you are looking at is a series of satellite photos taken by Argus," explained the captain. "They were linked together by our computer to form a continuity map that we could work from. The longitude and latitude lines are the computer's, too."

"What a mess!" said Tom, as he studied the abrupt surface contrasts of the moon. Captain Barrot and his father laughingly agreed.

"A perfect description," said the captain.

The irregularities in the features of the moon stood out in sharp contrast from one another. Craters, ringed with wide, bright halos of ice, lay next to broad, smooth plains. Next to that, regions of craggy mountains could be seen. A network of grooves and ridges, called *sulci*, branched and intersected throughout the area, evidence of Ganymede's history of violent surface activity resembling that of Earth. To top it all off, a blanket of ice, hundreds of kilometers thick, covered the entire territory.

Tom slowly shook his head. "Why pick such a rough site for our base of operations? There must be a more hospitable-looking moon circling Jupiter."

"There is," the captain explained. "Ganymede was chosen as a compromise. It is close enough to allow us to study Jupiter and the other moons yet far enough away to permit adequate, long-term shielding from the highly radioactive giant planet."

"Also its gravity is very close to that of Earth's Moon, so we can expect our equipment to function as well as it would there."

Rafe Barrot punched another code into the computer and on the wall screen a large crater jumped into view.

"We've chosen a site near the south pole on the dark side," he said, "next to the largest crater in the area, Gilgamesh. That way, we'll have more than enough space to land equipment and conduct experiments. We're looking at approximately sixty-five degrees west latitude, a hundred and thirty-seven degrees south longitude."

"And the *Daniel Boone*," Mr. Swift added, "in geosynchronous orbit with the dark side, will use the moon as a shield."

Rafe Barrot nodded. "We'll be going into Ganymede's orbit about three weeks from today," he said.

This is it, Tom thought, a shiver of excitement going through him. Soon mankind would set foot on the icy crust of another planet's moon for the first time—and he would be one of those history-making people!

Chapter Four

After their briefing by the captain, Tom left his father and, along with Ben, went to Anita's room in the Intensive Care ward of the ship's infirmary. "Anita," he called out softly, opening the door. There was no answer.

"Maybe she's asleep," whispered Ben.

Tom opened the door a bit wider and poked his head inside the room. "Anita?"

Suddenly there was a crash and the sound of glass breaking against the door. Tom withdrew his head quickly.

"Hey, you *could* have taken the flowers out of the vase first," he called through the now closed door. "I had quite a time getting the hydroponics people to give them to me!"

The hydroponics section of the *Daniel Boone* was mainly responsible for putting fresh oxygen into the ship's air-circulation system by growing a variety of plants, including flowers and fresh vegetables, in huge tanks of water and nutrients. In addition to the oxygen the plants gave off, there were other benefits as well. The fresh vegetables grown on the ship relieved the monotony of the freeze-dried food, and the occasional fresh flowers added brightness and color. The flowers, however, were a rarity, and very highly prized.

There was silence from inside Anita's room. Tom cautiously poked his head in again. The redhead was sitting up in bed and he could tell she was furious.

"Get out!" she yelled at him. "I told them I didn't want anyone to see me like this!"

"It's all right, Anita, I—"

Tom withdrew his head from the room abruptly, and both boys heard the sound of a solid object crash against the door.

"I guess that means she's not asleep after all," Ben quipped dryly.

"You and your old robot!" Anita grumbled. "I hope you all spring a leak in your space suits and choke!"

This time, Ben put his head into the room.

"You don't mean that, Anita—" A flying hair-brush narrowly missed his eye.

"I think she does," said Tom ruefully as Ben jumped back. The two boys looked at each other, helplessly.

"In a way, I can understand how she feels," said Tom. "She's on the greatest expedition in the history of mankind and she's confined to a bed. I'd be pretty mad, too, if it were me."

"I wish she'd let me see her leg," said Ben. "While you and your father were with the captain, I talked to Doctor Ling. He said that it was totally dead, but he's no computer expert. Other than that, she's all right. If I could just get a look at it, I might be able to help her walk again."

Just then, the doors of the elevator opened and Tom's father walked toward them.

"How's Anita?" he asked.

"She's pretty upset because she can't walk without crutches," Tom replied.

"Let me talk to her," said the elder Swift, opening the door as he spoke.

"Dad, I wouldn't—"

The boys heard the crash of glass against the door, then Anita gasped.

"Oh, Mister Swift," she cried. "I'm so sorry! I thought—oh, never mind what I thought!"

"I haven't been greeted that way since I was about Tom's age." Mr. Swift chuckled as he entered the room, followed cautiously by the two boys. He casually brushed water off his jumpsuit.

"I'm so sorry," Anita repeated. "I just let my emotions get away with me sometimes. It has all been so exciting, and now, just before we're about to land on Ganymede, *this* happens! I'm going to miss the rest of the trip!" The young girl burst into tears.

"Nonsense," said Mr. Swift. "Some of the finest minds in the scientific community are on board this ship, not to mention two members of the Swift family! Do you think for one minute that we would allow a valuable member of the team to spend the rest of the trip loafing in bed? Do you, young lady?"

Anita sniffed and blew her nose. Then she laughed self-consciously. "N-no, I guess I was being foolish."

"That's better," said the elder Swift. He turned and winked at the two boys.

"Do you feel up to a trip to the lab?" Tom asked Anita. "We haven't been down there since the accident."

"If you're sure I won't be in the way," the girl replied, but she was already getting out of bed. Tom reached over to help her with a pair of crutches that were leaning against a table.

"Just give me ten minutes to get dressed," she said excitedly. "Then we can be on our way."

Tom looked at the lab door in silence. He was almost afraid to open it, but he knew that his father, Ben, and Anita were waiting for him. He reached inside the steel panel recessed into the bulkhead and pushed the red handle up. Instantly he heard a hissing sound, as air was pumped back into the lab. A minute later, a buzzer sounded—the "all clear" signal—indicating the lab had been filled with air and the pressure equalized. Tom turned the wheel that unlocked the chamber and went in.

A layer of thick soot covered everything and felt sticky to the touch. It was the result of the melted plastic insulation that had become airborne during the fire.

The robot stood where it had been left. It, too, was coated with the sticky soot. Tom's heart fell as he saw that the only thing left of the arm were the steel struts. Metal globules from the bulkhead were melted onto it.

"I guess it's back to square one," Ben remarked dejectedly.

"Don't be too sure," Tom said. "I built this robot for outer space. In a strange way, this was a good test for it, because if it can't survive a fire in a laboratory, it's got no chance on a place like Io. The arm was unshielded and we'll definitely have to rebuild that, but the rest of it should be all right."

Tom brushed the soot off the light on the sensorframe. "There's still power inside," he announced.

"Congratulations, Son," said his father. "But you still have a lot of work ahead of you if you want to get the robot finished before we start setting up the Ganymede base."

"That's right," Tom agreed. He looked around the lab. How would they ever get it back into working condition? Most of the equipment, and all of Tom's personal tools, had been totally destroyed. And as soon as the *Daniel Boone* went into orbit around Ganymede, his father would count on both him and the robot to help build the base.

"You will need a place to work," said the elder Swift as if he had been reading Tom's thoughts. "It won't be worth your time to restore this lab. Come with me." The three young people followed Mr. Swift down the corridor and into the elevator. They went up two decks and through a long passageway.

"But—these are your private quarters, Dad!" exclaimed Tom, aghast.

"No, those are my private quarters," his father replied, pointing two hatches down from the one he was opening with a magnetic key. "This is my private lab."

When they were all inside, the three young people gasped in astonishment.

The blackness of space surrounded and enveloped them. Where the walls should have been, great crystal-clear panels of the strongest polyglas known to man had been set into the very framework of the giant ship.

"Jewels on dark velvet," said Tom, mesmerized by the millions of pinpoints of light all around them.

"We've really gone to the stars," Anita muttered. "We've been so busy since this trip started that I haven't had a chance to go up on the observation deck to look out. The inside of the ship has been my whole world. I forgot what it was like outside!"

The elder Swift smiled. "In a few minutes you'll see a real sight. We should be coming up on Jupiter."

"When you're in the ship you can't tell we're spinning," said Ben. The *Daniel Boone,* shaped like a giant cylinder, rotated on its axis once every 114 seconds. That gave its passengers a close approximation of Earth-normal gravity on the perimeter.

"It's funny how we humans use Earth to measure our lives," said Tom. "A day, for example, is twenty-four hours. But that's only because it takes our planet that long to make one complete revolution on its axis. On Ganymede, the days will be 168 hours long. Since it shows the same face to Jupiter all the time, its period of rotation is equal to its revolution about the planet."

"Or how about a year?" said Anita, frowning. "It takes Jupiter twelve Earth years to make one complete revolution around the Sun. A girl could sure age a lot in a year like that!" Suddenly she began to laugh and Tom, his father, and Ben joined in.

The hypnotic effect of the view from the lab had been broken by Anita's joke and the three young people looked around eagerly.

Every piece of testing equipment imaginable had been fitted into the room.

"Incredible!" exclaimed Tom. "We'd have to go all over the ship to find some of this stuff!"

"Help Anita onto the examining table, Son," said Mr. Swift. The young inventor put the girl's crutches aside and lifted her onto a big segmented table near the center of the lab. It was motorized and any part of it could be moved so that it was in exactly the right spot for any experiment.

The elder Swift motioned to Ben as he pulled a large machine on wheels out of a bank of other equipment. "Give me a hand with this, will you please?" he asked. Together they wheeled it over to where Tom and Anita were waiting.

"What's that?" Anita asked. The big machine had rows of dials and gauges, an alpha-numeric keyboard, and a blank screen that looked like a computer monitor.

"It's a general electronics testing peripheral," Tom explained. "The power source is the ship's computer, but the peripheral has its own programs for testing. It increases the versatility of our computer without a lot of new programing that nobody else would have a use for."

Ben quickly scanned the machine with professional interest. "I've never seen one quite like it," he said. "Normally it would take several pieces of equipment to get a really accurate reading like the one you can get on this."

"We planned for limited space on the *Daniel Boone*," said Tom's father. "This is one of the ways we did it."

When they had finished hooking up the machine to the ship's computer terminal in the lab, and had connected the tester's leads to Anita's wrist controller, Ben sat down in front of the tester's keyboard. He looked at Tom expectantly.

"We think that your computer's internal power source is dead, Anita, which is why you can't move your leg," said Tom. "Let's see if we can get a voltage pattern, just to make sure."

Ben worked over the keyboard for a moment. An oscilloscope grid flashed on the screen. Then a spot of light appeared at the zero line of the scope and stretched flat across the grid.

"No pattern," said Ben. "The power source was probably burned out by the high-voltage surge that occurred when you yanked the adapter lead out of the robot."

"I agree," said Tom. "Sensitive transistors, and especially diodes, don't like power surges."

"Oh, that's what you were trying to warn me about," Anita said sheepishly.

"I probably should have phrased my warning better," said Tom. He patted Anita on the shoulder.

"Put power to the central processing unit," Mr. Swift instructed. "Let's see if there's any continuity."

Ben did, then shrugged. "Nothing's coming out."

"Even the motherboard is junk," sighed the

redhead, referring to her computer's main circuit board. "That's the ball game."

"No, it's not!" Tom said firmly. "Ben and I reconstructed the *Davy Cricket* out of almost nothing after my original racer blew up! Our computer was sabotaged twice and we still made it into the race."

"And you won, too!" Anita smiled. "At least my *Valkyrie* came in second."

"I'm sure we can get you walking," Ben said.

"We can do more than that," chuckled Tom's father. The young people looked at him in surprise as he unlocked a sturdy metal closet and took out a black plastic box that fit in the palm of his hand. "Do you remember the micro-computer chip design we discussed over dinner several months ago, Tom?"

"Of course," Tom said excitedly. "I've been so busy with the robot that I forgot about it!"

Mr. Swift saw that Ben and Anita had puzzled expressions on their faces and smiled at them apologetically. "Tom and I came up with this after a minor accident that had taken place that afternoon in the nuclear research lab.

"The technicians were conducting final experiments on the decontamination solution that we needed on this expedition to combat Jupiter's radiation. They were behind safety shielding and were working with waldos to mix the solution in the experimental chamber—"

"Waldos are those robot arms that are used when it's not safe for humans to be close by, aren't they?" Anita asked.

"That's right," Tom said. "The techs were having trouble with the experiment because the waldos weren't sensitive enough. It took them longer than it should have to complete the experiment and they almost dropped one of the vials of solution."

"That night," Mr. Swift went on, "Tom and I decided we needed a more sensitive chip to control the movement of the waldos, so we designed it right there at the dinner table!"

"And Mom was upset because we let the roast beef get cold!" Tom chuckled.

Then he swallowed hard to control the pang of homesickness he felt every time he thought of his mother, back in New Mexico, waiting for her husband and her son who were quite literally a million miles away. Tom could tell that his father's thoughts were there, too.

The elder Swift opened the black plastic box and held it out for the three young people to see. A half-inch square of epoxy and metal lay inside. Tiny wires protruded from one edge of it.

"There's nothing inside the package," exclaimed Ben, using the technical name for the tiny epoxy square.

"Yes, there is," Mr. Swift replied, and motioned for the boys to follow him to a workbench that had a huge microscope on it. He opened the instrument drawer and selected a pair of forceps. Then, slowly and carefully, he took the epoxy square out of the box and placed it under the microscope. "Take a look," he said.

"You go first, Ben," Tom said to his friend. It was obvious that the young Indian was excited by the new micro-computer chip. He had an almost uncanny ability with computers and, in Tom's opinion, Benjamin Franklin Walking Eagle was the foremost expert on the latest in computer hardware.

Ben peered intently through the microscope. He was silent for a few seconds, then stood up with a look of pure rapture on his face. "Now that's what I call beautiful!" he said, breaking into a wide grin. He stepped aside to let Tom have a look.

"It needs to be tested in a working situation," said Tom's father, looking directly at Anita. "I'd like you to put it to the test, Ms. Thorwald."

Anita was embarrassed for a moment, then she smiled shyly. "I can hardly refuse an offer like that, Mister Swift, but Tom needs all his time for

the robot. He'll be running all over the ship between the two projects, and he might not get the
robot finished before we get to Ganymede."

Mr. Swift turned to his son. "After you've fixed
Anita's leg, bring the robot up here. I'm not going to work much in this lab from now on. I need
to help Rafe Barrot plan the setup of the Ganymede base."

"How are we going to move the robot?" Tom
asked.

"You can borrow a chain hoist and a cart from
the people down in Cargo. Then you can wheel
the monster up here," his father replied. "If the
chip proves successful in Anita's leg, Ben can put
together another one for the robot."

Tom grinned at Anita. "That way we can get
both you and the robot in top form before we set
up base. Whoever would have thought we would
have such a cute guinea pig for our micro-computer chip?" he added slyly.

"You just wait, Tom Swift," the redhead exploded. "You're lucky there's no vase here! I
have a good mind to—" she broke off abruptly.

"Look!" she pointed.

Chapter Five

In the forward window of the lab, the brightly colored surface of Jupiter appeared. They all stared in utter silence at the awesome sight.

"It's truly breathtaking," Mr. Swift finally said quietly. "And to think that those of us on the *Daniel Boone* are the first people in history to see it like this."

"It won't be long now before we will swing close to Ganymede and begin to set up our base," said Tom. "We'd better get cracking or we'll never be ready in time."

During the next few days, the young people spent all their waking moments in the lab Tom's father had allowed them to use. The robot had 51 been moved into it and the facility had become home to them.

After putting her leg through every test she could think of, Anita announced the micro-computer chip had passed them all. Ben promptly set to work making a copy of the chip for the robot.

The day it was finally finished, the two boys headed out from their quarters to the laboratory.

"I still don't believe it," exclaimed Ben. "There must be a way to find out what caused the robot to malfunction. There had to be some reason."

Tom shrugged and smiled apologetically at his friend. "We ran the robot's complete program and did circuit checks on every part of it. Nothing showed up. The rebuilt arm checks out perfectly and it hasn't malfunctioned since we reactivated our friend. The only conclusion I can draw is that the bug that caused the accident was somewhere in the arm that got burned up."

Anita looked up from a microfiche viewer as the two boys entered the lab. "Hi," she said.

Next to her, the robot turned the domed center of its sensorframe until the deep blue-violet "eyes" of its two camera lenses were directed at Tom. It watched the young inventor as he moved around the lab.

The robot's sensorframe had been completed

just a few days before. It was obvious, however, that the mechanoid already had a definite preference of its camera "sight" over sonarscan and the photosensitive arrays. Was it a quirk of the central processing unit? Tom was not sure. It was, however, the kind of "personality trait" he had hoped for in the robot. The element of random choice. A human quality. It made the robot more than a mere machine.

Today would mark the beginning of a new phase in Tom's relationship with his creation. The new micro-computer chip had been mounted in its package and would be connected to its printed-circuit card, called the PC card.

Its AUDIGEN—AUDIo GENerator—circuit manufactured the voice. Communication with the robot would no longer be restricted to task-oriented commands, such as instructing the elevator to go to the bridge. The AUDIGEN circuit in the recently completed micro-computer chip was the most sophisticated one to be attempted. If it was successful, talking with the robot would be much like talking with another human being!

"How did Ben take the news about the burned-up bug?" asked Anita.

"It was traumatic for him, but he'll pull through," answered Tom, grinning at his friend.

Ben shook his head, obviously amused.

"It's pretty hard even for me to accept the fact that we were almost killed by some electronic 'glitch' that we never found," Anita said. "It does seem to be the only answer, though."

Tom grimaced. "The idea of being haunted by this for the rest of my life doesn't appeal to me. I'll never know what I did wrong. I hate to make mistakes, but when I do, I like to correct them and learn from the experience."

"And we have no way of knowing when or if the malfunction will raise its ugly head again," Anita said. "Do you suppose we have a robot we can't trust?"

The three young people looked at each other in silence for a moment. It was a question they had each asked themselves many times.

Ben shrugged, breaking the somber mood that had descended upon the group. "We used the computer to check everything out. If computers don't lie, then we have nothing to worry about. And you both know how I stand on that subject."

"Besides," Tom said, "the whole space program has been plagued by 'glitches' since it started. A lot of the early launches were postponed for hours—and even days—because some cheap valve didn't work. It's all part of the exploration game!"

"Look," Anita broke in, "could we change the subject? We never really came to any conclusions about whether the robot listens to us when we talk about it, or even if it's capable of anything approaching an emotional reaction because of what it hears. But I can't shake the uncomfortable feeling that we're gossiping about someone right in front of him."

"Him?" Ben asked laughing.

"Well . . . it. Him. Whatever," Anita said with some hesitation. "It makes me feel strange."

Tom smiled at Anita, surprised at the emotion in her voice. She looked away hurriedly.

"I'm—I'm sorry," she mumbled. "I know it's silly, but—"

"We've all been working too hard," said Tom. "You and Ben and I ought to take a break. I know, let's go to the hub and get some exercise before we start back to work."

The hub was the center axis of the giant spaceship. Because of the rotation of the *Daniel Boone,* the middle of the ship enjoyed weightlessness. For the amusement and the health of those on board, the hub had been sectioned off into athletic courts where several different kinds of null-gravity sports were played.

Anita's face instantly brightened at Tom's suggestion. "I haven't been up there since the accident! Now that your new micro-computer chip is in my leg, you are really going to have one formidable opponent!" She laughed at the expression on Tom's face.

"When you asked me to test your chip, I bet you didn't think it might ruin your record in null-gravity handball, did you!"

Ben and Tom looked at each other in mock dismay.

"We need another person if we're going to play null-gravity handball," said Ben.

Tom smiled devilishly. "And I know just who to ask, too—my father."

"Oh, no," Anita protested. "That will give you an unfair advantage!" She knew of the elder Swift's reputation, even though he had only been playing for a short time. Tom had introduced him to it on their last trip to the *New America* space colony, and his father had shown an enviable natural ability for the game.

Anita's mood changed so abruptly that it caught Tom off guard. "You haven't seen much of your father these past few weeks, and it bothers you, doesn't it? You're very worried about him."

"I—I suppose so," said Tom, feeling uncomfortable. It was as if the young woman had looked into the most private and secret corner of his heart.

He *had* been worried about his father, who had a habit of overworking himself in critical situations. On Earth, he had his secretary, Marguerite, and his chief assistant, Gene Larson, to stop him from doing that. But they were now on the *Daniel Boone.* Frankly, Tom had been feeling guilty about spending so much time working, and very little checking up on his father, even though the elder Swift would never have tolerated being checked up on by his son.

"You shouldn't feel guilty," said Anita.

"How did you know what I was thinking?" asked Tom.

"I didn't," replied Anita. She looked at Tom with a puzzled expression on her face. "All of a sudden, I could just tell what you were feeling. Not thinking, feeling. The odd part of it is, I don't know how I knew. I don't know why I feel the way I do about the robot, either. I just do. Sometimes it's eerie. I wish I understood it all a little bit better."

Tom looked at the robot and caught his breath. His eyes met the unblinking camera lenses. It *is* more than just a machine, he thought to himself. He turned back to Anita and put a hand on her shoulder.

"Before we go play some championship handball, let's install the new chip with the AUDIGEN circuit so we can find out just what the robot does think," he suggested.

Anita smiled up at him and nodded. Ben eagerly agreed.

Tom knew the AUDIGEN circuit he had designed would put a big load on the robot's central processing unit. Usually, AUDIGEN was delegated to TTL circuitry—transistor-transistor logic. That way, the central processing unit, or "brain" of a computer or robot, could concentrate on higher-level duties. That was how the AUDIGEN circuit of the *Daniel Boone's* elevator worked.

Tom walked over to the workbench where Ben was holding a small soldering iron with a needle-fine tip in his hand. He was peering through an adjustable magnifying glass at a thin, rectangular wafer of metal. Through the magnifying glass, Tom could see the tiny lines, or traces, of the electrical circuits that had been photographically etched into the wafer. Ben touched the point of the soldering iron to the wafer near the base of the epoxy square that had been mounted in the center of it. A thin column of smoke rose from the place the iron had touched. He pushed the magnifying glass down closer and double-checked his work. Then he sat back and looked at Tom with a satisfied expression on his face.

"The chip's mounted," he said.

"Let's get it in, then," said Tom. He picked up the small, printed-circuit card with a pair of forceps and walked over to the robot.

"Unlock the control unit," he said to the mechanoid.

There was a clicking sound and then the whir of a tiny electric motor. A drawer-like section came forward out of the robot's chest.

Five PC cards were standing upright in the drawer, and there was a place for a sixth. Tom inserted the new card into the empty spot, using the forceps. He was careful not to touch any of the other cards with his hands as perspiration could damage the electrical components.

"Lock the controls," he said to the robot when he was satisfied that the card was connected properly. The electric motor pulled the drawer back into the mechanoid's chest. It locked with a faint click.

There was a scratching sound that resembled some of the old recordings made on plastic discs that Tom's father had played for him when he was very young. Then, in a emotionless, electronic voice, the robot said, "Control unit . . . locked . . . Tom."

Tom, Ben, and Anita were stunned. No one spoke for a few seconds. They just stared at the robot in awe.

Finally, Tom broke the silence. "I designed him to talk, I built him to talk, and now I can't believe he can talk!"

Ben laughed. "The inventor is overwhelmed by his invention. Say something to . . . ah, I guess we have to say 'him,' don't we? Certainly a robot who can talk is more than a machine, more than an 'it.' Say something to *him,* Tom."

But Tom couldn't think of anything to say!

The silence grew awkward, then he finally mumbled, "Hello, robot."

"Hello . . . Tom," replied the robot.

Behind him, Anita started to giggle. She stopped when the mechanoid turned to her and asked, "Anita . . . functioning . . . well?"

"He spoke to me!" she gasped.

Tom felt a twinge of apprehension that had been nagging at him since he started the robot project. It was the fear of unleashing something on the world over which he, as inventor, had no control. The robot had spoken without being asked a question, and Tom knew that he had invented a mechanical "being" that could think for itself far more independently than its limited program.

Could the robot willingly do violence to a human? No. Tom had made very sure of that. Still, the thought of coexisting with a robot that had an unpredictable personality was a bit scary. It would take getting used to.

"We can't go on calling him 'robot,' you know," said Ben. "He should have a name."

Tom nodded. "I've been thinking about that."

"What about an acronym like 'Tom's Intelligent Machine.' That's 'TIM,' " suggested Ben.

"Somehow, that's not dignified enough," Tom objected.

"Wait a minute, you two," Anita broke in. "After all the time and effort to make the robot think, don't you believe it is only fair that he should have some choice in selecting his name? After all, it is *his* name!"

Tom grinned, "You are absolutely correct, Anita." He turned to the robot. "Okay, robot. What would you like your name to be?"

The robot was silent for a moment and then his head swiveled from side to side. "No . . . Tom. The . . . creator . . . has the . . . right . . . to name the . . . result of his . . . labors." Then it fell silent.

"So much for that idea," Tom sighed.

"You can always pick a name out of mythology," said Ben. "Call him Hercules, or something."

"That doesn't sound right either." Tom frowned in thought. "He's too intellectual for that. In fact, I've been thinking of calling him Aristotle, after my favorite Greek philosopher."

"Aristotle?" asked Anita.

"Please to meet you, Aristotle," said Ben to the robot.

"I am greatly—" The robot paused for a few seconds, then said, "I have no word in my vocabulary bank. My components are in harmonious synchronization with the name, Aristotle."

Tom smiled. "Humans often make comparisons in terms of pleasure and pain, Aristotle. Pleasure is harmonious synchronization, pain is the opposite."

"I am—pleased," said Aristotle.

"This calls for a celeb—" Tom was cut off in mid-sentence by the loud, high-pitched wail of the ship's siren.

"What's wrong?" Anita cried out.

Chapter Six

Tom listened to the high-pitched whine of the siren for a moment. An expression of great relief crossed his face.

"Nothing's wrong," he said, excitedly. "That's just the signal that we're now entering Ganymede orbit! Let's go down to the recreation room and watch."

The three young people ran for the lab hatch. Ben and Anita ducked through first and their footsteps echoed down the corridor. Tom paused at the hatch. "Come on, Aristotle! I don't want your sensors to miss this!"

Aristotle moved forward a few inches, then 63

stopped. Tom grimaced impatiently. "What's wrong?" he asked.

"I am a faulty mechanism," replied the robot.

Tom straightened up and stared at the robot. "Explain," he said, formally.

"During my construction, I malfunctioned and caused the human, Anita, to break down. The cause of the malfunction is unknown, therefore, the probability exists that I may again go against my programing, as you stated, Tom."

So the robot *had* heard and stored everything he, Ben, and Anita had said about it! What was more, the information had been interpreted on a level that Tom had not thought would be possible. He now had a robot with a guilt complex!

Tom grinned. "I require that you come with me to the recreation room, Aristotle. We'll discuss your malfunction later." He knew that the robot *could not* disobey a direct order.

"Yes, Tom," Aristotle replied, moving forward again, this time without hesitation.

The *Daniel Boone's* rec room was packed by the time the young people and Aristotle arrived. Scientists, technicians, and civilians were conversing excitedly. Tom noticed many navy uniforms in the crowd, which was very unusual.

A few people stared at Aristotle, but most everyone's attention was focused on the excitement of the moment.

Besides, robots were not all that unusual a sight for the scientists and technicians of the *Daniel Boone*. Some were in storage in the ship's hold. They would be an important part of the work force at the Ganymede base. They were not, however, as sophisticated as Aristotle.

Tom saw his father at the opposite end of the room, near the giant wall screen normally used for computer games. Suddenly, Captain Rafe Barrot's voice come over the loudspeaker.

The room quieted instantly as the captain gave orders to the bridge crew. It must be very busy up there, Tom thought, as he listened to the sound of the *Daniel Boone's* instruments and of the crew performing their assigned duties.

Then, quite suddenly, the wall screen sprang into life with a spectacular view of Ganymede, framed by the huge, marbled surface of Jupiter. Tom had never seen anything more beautiful— or more alien.

For one thing, his mind boggled at the proportions. It was not like looking at Earth from the Moon, as he had done while visiting Armstrong base. Jupiter was about thirteen hundred times larger than Earth!

Of course Tom knew that they were seeing

only the violently swirling upper atmosphere of the planet. A short distance below that gaseous layer was a liquid hydrogen sea, and below that, it was believed, lay a small rocky core about the size of Earth.

A cheer went up from the people in the room as four tiny orbiting specks suddenly came into view at Ganymede's equator—the equipment pods sent from Earth months ago! They had survived the rigors of space and the hazards of attaining Ganymede orbit. All of the equipment in the pods would be needed to construct the Ganymede base.

Despite the work he and Swift Enterprises had put into this project, Tom still felt a lump in his throat at the wonder of it all. Seeing those tiny man-made objects floating against the vastness of space, taking their places exactly as planned between the immenseness of Jupiter and its circling moon gave Tom a thrill as great as the time he had hit a grand slam home run back on Earth.

Abruptly, he felt a small change in the ship's rhythm. It was so subtle that he was surprised he had noticed it at all.

After a moment, the rhythm changed again. Tom looked at Ben and Anita. They had felt it, too.

"The sequence of deceleration maneuvers for

geosynchronous orbit has begun, Tom," Aristotle spoke up.

Tom looked at the robot in amazement.

He was right. The *Daniel Boone* had been in deceleration for several weeks now, but geosynchronous orbit meant that the ship would decelerate to match the exact orbital speed of Ganymede as the moon traveled around Jupiter.

Like the Earth's Moon, the Galilean satellites presented the same face toward Jupiter. That was extremely important to the location of the Ganymede base because of the tremendous radiation given off by Jupiter. The base would be located near the south pole of Ganymede, on the dark side. The *Daniel Boone* would use the moon as a shield and would never be out of communication with the base. It was all very neat and carefully thought out. Tom hoped it worked as well in practice as it did in theory.

When the excitement over entering Ganymede's orbit had died down, the rec room emptied slowly. Tom, his father, his friends, and his robot headed for the hub for the game of null-gravity handball which they had planned to play. The place was almost deserted and they had no trouble finding an available court.

"Everyone's probably enjoying their last few hours of full gravity," Ben remarked.

"You stay here and watch, Aristotle," Tom instructed. "I doubt you are up to this sort of activity."

Anita pushed off from the wall near the entry hatch and turned three graceful somersaults in midair. She finished with a half-twist and floated over to join Ben on the far side of the court. They would be a team.

"Beautifully done," exclaimed Tom.

"Your leg appears to be functioning rather well," said the elder Swift.

"The new chip in it is much more responsive than the old one," Anita said. "I tried a few ballet steps last night and I was able to do some things I've never been able to do before. The chip's sensitivity is so uncanny it is almost scary."

"Enough talk, you," said Tom teasingly. "Let's start playing!" He floated into position next to his father.

The court was a large geodesic globe with triangular windows. Areas inside the globe were painted green, blue, yellow, and black. A thick, red line bisected the globe into two hemispheres, and it was back and forth across this line the players leaped and plunged.

Each of the black areas, which were off limits to both sides, had an electronic sensor mat under it, so there was no need to call the shot. Each team had its own color and could be penalized one point for touching the opponent's color.

The ball had to rebound from the opposite hemisphere from which it began, before a hit could be scored. A sensor inside the ball helped in calling close plays, as did the hair-line sensor in the red line.

"Ready," Tom called to the wall speaker. A circular hatch on the red line opened and a black ball shot out. The gaming computer controlled the direction of the ball, but the choice was random. This time, the ball flew toward Anita's and Ben's side of the court and bounced off the wall.

"It's mine," said Tom's father, and he launched himself into the air gracefully. He met the ball and hurled it toward Ben. The equal and opposite reaction of the movement sent him backward. He used the force for a perfect back-flip and landed on his side of the court again.

Ben watched the ball bounce, then he sent it back to Tom and his father.

"Mine," said Tom. He leaped into the air to meet the ball—and knew he wasn't going to catch it. It had been too long since he had played the game and he was out of practice. He had mis-judged the speed of the ball and had overshot the point where he should have made contact with it. The ball went past him and he sailed awkwardly into a penalty area.

Tom felt foolish as he floated back into position for the next round. He glanced at Anita and was startled to see that she was staring at him, with an intense expression on her face that he had never seen before. It made him very uneasy.

The computer put the ball into play again and this time it shot within striking range of Mr. Swift. He sent it over to Ben and Anita by "express." This ball stayed in play for quite a few minutes before Ben missed it, giving Tom and his father a point.

Anita was still watching Tom. It made him uncomfortable and a little angry, too. It seemed as though she were concentrating her game on him.

Well, he would show her that she couldn't get to him!

The computer picked Ben and Anita again. Anita watched the ball bounce off the court wall, then she leaped up and met it expertly, sending it straight to Tom.

The young inventor dived to get out of the way of the projectile by pushing against the nearest wall. The reaction sent him backward, out of control. He struck the court head first and pain shot through him. At that moment, he heard

Anita cry out! He forgot about his head and looked at her in surprise.

Tom's father and Ben were already holding on to Anita when Tom reached her. She seemed to be in pain, but no one had seen her get hurt.

"What happened?" Tom asked anxiously. "How did she hurt herself?"

"She didn't," said Ben. "I don't understand it! I saw you hit the wall and then she yelled."

"I—I was watching you," said Anita, "and I knew you were going to miss the point—I knew that *you* knew you would, too. When you hit the wall, I got a sharp pain in my head! Can someone please tell me what's happening to me? I seem to be picking up signals from other people whether I want to or not. And I'm not sure I like it at all!"

"Have there been other incidents like this one?" Tom's father asked, alarmed.

Tom filled him in briefly on Anita's strange experiences since the accident. The elder Swift frowned as he listened to his son.

"Let's go down to the lab. I have a theory, but I want to run some tests before I say what I think the problem is."

Once in the lab, Tom and Ben helped Anita onto the examining table while Mr. Swift got the computer test peripheral they had used to examine her the first time. No one spoke as he finished hooking it up to the test connectors on Anita's new leg. In the background, Aristotle watched the humans.

Mr. Swift punched up a series of electrical tests on the console. He looked at the data on the CRT—the cathode-ray-tube computerscreen—and frowned.

It was the kind of frown that scientists made when they found something that they hoped they wouldn't find, even though it meant they were right. Tom knew, because he had frowned that way many times.

"Anita is getting electrical feedback through the central processing unit in her artificial leg," Mr. Swift declared. "It's having an unusual effect on her nervous system."

"It's the new chip," Tom said.

Ben looked puzzled. "You mean, some electronic feedback means she can tell what someone else is going to do or what they are feeling?"

Mr. Swift nodded. "It is an area scientists have long been interested in but one in which little concrete research has been done up until now." He turned to the redheaded girl. "With your permission, we might be able to learn a lot about the relationship between emotions, thoughts, and electrical impulses."

Before the young girl could respond the robot spoke.

"Anita has malfunctioned?" asked Aristotle.

The elder Swift turned toward the robot and then looked questioningly at Tom.

"Humans don't malfunction, Aristotle," said Tom. "They get sick, or hurt, or angry, sad or happy, but they don't malfunction."

"My circuits exchanged current with Anita. A malfunction occurred in her circuits at that time. Please explain, Tom."

Tom heard his father whistle softly between his teeth. "Congratulations," the elder Swift whispered to his son. "Aristotle is an amazing scientific invention, and is certainly living up to his name!"

Tom looked at the robot in silence for a few seconds. This was going to be difficult.

"Humans don't malfunction, Aristotle," said Tom. "Anita is a special human. She's—"

"I'm part robot, Aristotle," interrupted Anita. Her remark caught Tom totally off guard.

"It is the best way to explain it to him," Anita insisted to the others. She turned back to Aristotle. "I had an accident when I was younger and the doctors had to amputate the lower part of my right leg. A computer brain 'translates' signals from my brain to the working parts of the artificial leg so that I can walk."

"I caused this part of you to malfunction," Aristotle stated. "You are having difficulty which I caused. I was not programed to cause discomfort to humans. I am an imperfect mechanism."

"*Aristotle!*" yelled Tom, alarmed. "Stop that! It's not true!"

"It is fact," said the robot, stubbornly. "Truth is that which conforms with fact and reality. You are in error, Tom."

"You've been out-argued by your own programing," chortled Ben. "This is the kind of thing we computer people love!"

"You're not helping, Ben," said Tom, exasperated. Then he turned to his father. "Don't just sit there, help me!"

"Who am I to interfere between the creator and his creation?" asked the elder Swift, grinning mischievously.

"Thanks a lot!" said Tom, but he could not help a smile as the humor of the situation began to dawn on him. "Aristotle, sometimes the truth can be seen in different ways. . . ."

"Then it is not the truth, it is opinion," the robot retorted. "I am programed to know the difference between truth and opinion."

"You're wrong, Aristotle!"

"That is possible. I am a faulty mechanism."

Tom's mouth fell open with astonishment. He'd been trapped. He looked at Ben for help, but the computer tech was laughing so hard that tears were running down his cheeks. Anita and his father were trying not to join in, but Tom could tell they were losing control, too. He sat down, not knowing what to do.

"Okay, you've won this round, chum," he admitted.

Aristotle was silent and unmoving, but somehow, Tom was sure the robot was laughing, too!

Chapter Seven

It seemed as if everyone in the entire ship had gathered in the shuttle bay to send off the first of the lander craft to Ganymede's surface. For much of the voyage, speculation about the crew for this historic journey had been at a fever pitch. To be one of the first people to set foot on a moon of Jupiter would be a high honor.

Part of the crew had been selected according to the jobs which would have to be started immediately. The equipment pods circling the moon needed to be brought down and unloaded. The ice which covered the moon's surface had to be first leveled, then removed in big, square blocks.

After that, freezer coils would be laid and the ice blocks replaced. Heat sensors from the ice would activate the freezer coils when the ice was in danger of melting. One of the problems with trying to build a home on ice was that body heat and activity tended to melt it.

The buildings would be formed by inflating a huge plastic "balloon" which would act as a foundation to the dome. Once the balloon was inflated, the crew would spray plastic foam over it. After the foam hardened, the balloon would be removed, and support structures would be placed inside for safety. Next would come the airlock, then the entire structure had to be decontaminated and "scrubbed" of radiation.

The construction crew supervisor and his top three assistants would be on the first trip, as would the communications team who would be responsible for guiding the pods down safely.

But there were eight places on the historical team which would be made up from the *Daniel Boone's* crew at large. Those people would help with the physical labor involved in setting up the base.

It had been decided the fairest way to determine the rest of the team would be by random selection. A computer program was devised which would select the names from a list submitted. Everyone who wanted to go was instructed to type their names into the computer.

Tom, Anita, Ben, and Aristotle had all done so.

Captain Rafe Barrot stepped to the microphone. "I know all of you are anxious to learn who the computer has selected to be the first work crew. In the interest of fairness, I want to stress again that each member of the computer department cross-checked the program to make certain it was not rigged in any way."

Ben nudged Tom and said softly, "I checked it myself, just to be sure."

Anita moved a little closer to Aristotle. "Maybe we will all get to go."

"That would be a fortunate occurrence, but one that is mathematically improbable," the robot replied.

Captain Barrot continued. "Before I read the names, I remind you that everyone on the *Daniel Boone* will have a chance to go to Ganymede before we return home. We will work around the clock while building the base. Work cycles will be twelve hours long. In fact," he smiled, "I dare say that before many work cycles have been completed, most of you will be so tired you will wish you had never heard of Ganymede."

Everyone laughed.

"Now for the names of the lucky eight: Peter Elvino, Linda Stephenson, Ben Walking Eagle—"

Ben's face split into a wide grin and both Tom and Anita thumped him on the back.

"—Harrison Maney, Ruby von Mengden, Thor Lokvig, George Kalogeropoulous, and Tom Swift."

"Hey!" Ben said. "Two of us made it! That's great!"

Tom turned to Anita and Aristotle, "I'm sorry all of us couldn't go together."

"Oh, that's okay," Anita replied. "Aristotle and I will stay here and make sure the two of you do your jobs properly."

The boys moved to the dock where the lander craft was awaiting its crew. After slipping into the protective suits provided for the work teams, they climbed inside.

Moments later the little ship shot into space. Tom and Ben peered eagerly through their viewport, watching the moon grow larger. "Well, buddy, this is it!" Tom said.

The ship landed with a thud which they felt through the thick layers of insulation of radiation shielding of their suits.

"Let's go," cried Ben. "Time to conquer another frontier of space!"

By the end of the week, Tom, Ben, Anita, and Aristotle had all worked on Ganymede for a number of cycles and were ready to start another one.

"Where, oh where is the romance of space?" Tom heard Ben groan into his suit radio.

He undid the safety harness and stood up stiffly. He had not gotten enough sleep after yesterday's work at the base, or the time before that. Where was the romance of space, indeed. Commuting from the *Daniel Boone* to Ganymede at the beginning and end of each of the long, taxing work cycles was certainly getting to be a bore!

It did no good to complain, however. Everyone in the expedition had been pressed into hard labor. The domes had to be erected as soon as possible so that the scientists could live at the base instead of continuously shuttling from the ship. Fortunately, the main dome would be formed today. That was a major accomplishment, considering the expedition crew's state of fatigue.

Tom looked over at Aristotle. "Let's go," he said, and watched as the robot unfastened his own safety harness. Tom was still amazed at how nimble Aristotle's mechanical fingers were.

The young inventor motioned to Ben and Anita, then drifted out of the hatch of the shuttle ship in the slow, graceful stride that had been made famous by the first astronauts on the Earth's Moon. The waltz in one-sixth G! That was the gravity of both the Earth's Moon, and of Jupiter's Ganymede. The only difference was that the surface of Earth's Moon was fine dust. On Ganymede, everyone wore cleated boots that gripped the dirty ice surface. Even Aristotle had cleats on his traction pads, although the robot's tremendous weight helped to stabilize him, too.

Tom turned to make sure that Ben, Anita, and Aristotle were following him, then lumbered toward the cluster of lights that illuminated the partially constructed base camp. No one said anything. They were too tired for conversation.

Tom Swift looked upward. Since Ganymede had no atmosphere, the sky was not blue, even though it was officially "noon," Ganymede time. The stars in the blackness of space did not even twinkle on this airless world. And now there was a new object up there, the spaceship *Daniel Boone*. Tom sighed wistfully. It was going to be a long work cycle.

A suited, thick-set figure waved at him from the base camp perimeter. The suits, with their inch-thick powdered lead shielding, made everyone look a little heavy, but Tom still recognized the person from her body language.

Since suits masked facial expressions, exaggerated body language had become an important part of communication. Tom was amazed at how important it was—even with the suit radios. It put feeling and emotion into simple conversations that the radios seemed to take out.

The person holding up three fingers and waving at him was Dr. Fiona Friedman, a member of the astronomy team that had come to study the Great Red Spot of Jupiter. Tom switched his suit radio to channel three, the personal communications channel.

"Your father's looking for you, Tom," said the scientist in a worried tone. "He needs your help. Equipment pod number four won't come down and it's got a vital instrument package aboard plus some building materials that the dome crew needs immediately. You and Aristotle had better 'hot foot' it to the main dome site."

"Thanks, Doctor Friedman," Tom said. "We'll run right over there."

Dr. Friedman laughed and made an "okay" sign with her thickly gloved fingers.

Tom turned to his friends, but Ben motioned for him to go on.

"We heard the whole thing," the computer tech said. "Anita and I have to report to our work teams now, so we'll catch you later. Maybe we can all sit around and sip nutrient together."

Tom shrugged his shoulders to let Ben know that he wasn't thrilled about having a liquid lunch in his suit, either. Going back up to the ship would take too long, however, so they had no choice.

He watched as Ben and Anita veered off in another direction, then motioned for Aristotle to follow him. Together, they entered the lighted work area.

A surface rover pulled up next to Tom, and he recognized his father. The elder Swift held up one finger. That was the most private communications channel. The situation must be pretty serious, Tom thought.

"I'll drive you and Aristotle to the site where we've been bringing the pods down," said his father. "Number four isn't responding and, without our equipment from the *Daniel Boone,* we can't figure out exactly why. Maybe Aristotle can get it down."

"What's in the pod?" asked Tom.

"Most of the astronomy team's long-range observation equipment and the building materials for their dome."

Even over the suit radio, Tom could tell his father was worried.

"Have you analyzed the cause of this difficulty?" asked Aristotle. Tom realized with a start that it was the first time Aristotle had spoken in hours.

"As best we can figure out without more sophisticated equipment, something seems to have gone wrong with the pod's receiver," Mr. Swift replied. "Too much resistance could have caused the transmitted ground signal to be too weak. We need you to boost it, Aristotle."

"I shall do what I can," the robot promised. He and Tom got into the rover and traveled the rest of the way in silence.

On the ship, Aristotle had grown quite talkative as his vocabulary increased. The machine-mind was fascinating and Aristotle's learning capacity was astounding. But since the landing on Ganymede, the robot had talked less and less. It had gotten to the point where he only responded to direct questions.

Mechanically, he was functioning perfectly and he was an important member of the work crew. The spacesuits were clumsy and inhibited the humans in tasks that required nimbleness. Aristotle came in very handy in those instances, because he was not limited by a suit.

But why had he been so quiet lately? Tom was growing increasingly concerned, but he was too busy to try and do anything about the strange behavior. Maybe the mechanoid was just moody, he thought. But what would make a robot moody?

Presently, a group of suited figures came into view. They were clustered around a large portable transmitter whose antenna was fully extended. They waved as the Swifts' rover approached.

Tom recognized Dr. Harold Friedman among the group. The Friedmans had virtually uprooted themselves to join the Jupiter expedition. Their two sons, Ian and John, astronomers like their parents, made up the rest of the team. They had sold all their property and possessions to help finance the expedition, and while Harold and Fiona had university positions waiting for them upon their return to Earth, their reputation was at stake. The equipment on pod number four could literally make or break them.

"We want you to bring the pod down as close to this point as possible, Aristotle," said Tom. "Doctor Friedman will give you the code."

The rotund astronomer punched out the code signal on the transmitter. Aristotle "listened" without comment. "I am ready, Tom," he said, when Dr. Friedman had finished.

"Transmit the signal," Tom commanded.

"Transmitting," said the robot. "The signal has been received, Tom. The pod's landing sequence has begun."

There was a cheer from the astronomers, followed by much handshaking. Aristotle got a pat on the mainframe, too, as the group waited for the pod to come down.

"Good work," Tom praised the robot. He was proud of the expressionless mechanoid.

"The pod has not yet landed," the robot cautioned.

The comment caught Tom by surprise. He had come to recognize Aristotle's "moods" by the way he phrased things. It was not at all like him to be negative.

Tom's thoughts were interrupted by Dr. Friedman's shouts.

"I see it," the scientist called out, pointing skyward. "Here it comes."

But Tom knew something was wrong. The pod was coming in too fast. "Signal the pod to abort the landing and to try again," he told the robot.

"Transmitting," said Aristotle. "My signal has not been received, Tom."

Tom bit his lip in frustration, and everyone watched the pod speed past overhead toward the icy surface of Ganymede. Seconds later, a cry went up from the team. The pod had exploded, hurling ice and rock skyward!

While the Friedmans looked at each other dejectedly, Tom turned to Aristotle. "You did the best you could," he said.

"But I am, after all, a flawed mechanism," the robot replied.

As soon as communications were flashed to the main work area, Ben and Anita were reassigned to help Tom and Aristotle recover the pod.

The four drove over the rough, ice-covered surface of Ganymede in a surface rover, headed in the general direction of the crash site.

"Try veering left," said Ben.

Tom Swift turned the thick steering wheel counterclockwise. The rover responded sluggishly and he had to fight the wheel to maneuver a few degrees to the left of their present course.

"What does the detector read now?" he asked, without taking his eyes from the terrain ahead.

"There's a slight change in the rate of the light's pulsations," the computer tech answered. "They're definitely faster."

"Go more to the left," Anita advised. She was sitting in the back seat of the rover, next to the robot. "According to what you saw, the equipment pod can't be too far away."

"I am receiving a confused sonarscan reading," Aristotle spoke up. "My signals are bounding off some rough surface formations ahead of us."

"Thanks," said Tom. "Keep scanning anyway."

"I'm glad you volunteered us for this mission, Tom," Anita declared. "I needed a break from the labor camp! If I have to spread one more tank of dome foam, I'll go nuts!"

The young inventor laughed. "I hate it, too," he said. "Unfortunately, thanks to the crash landing of pod number four, we may have one less dome to construct. As much as I dislike the hard work, I hope, for the Friedmans' sake, that some of their stuff survived."

"What will they do if all their equipment is destroyed?" asked Ben.

"They'll still be able to carry on a few of their experiments," Tom replied, "but the expedition will pretty much be a disaster for them. They can do short-range observation, but that's about it."

"If that's the case, we won't be able to find out what happened to the Argus probe, will we?" Anita said. It was more a statement than a question. "Doctor Friedman was counting on the equipment to locate Argus."

"That's right," Tom agreed. "They had quite a series of experiments planned for Io and the flux tube."

"The flux tube is that weird magnetic effect between Io and Jupiter, isn't is?" Ben asked.

Tom nodded.

Ben checked the detector. "The signal is getting stronger," he said. "We're coming very close."

Tom peered into the distance. There was no sign of wreckage.

"I suggest we reduce our speed, Tom," said Aristotle. "I do not like the readings I am getting here."

Tom eased off the accelerator and the compact electric vehicle slowed down. The ride *had* been getting rougher as the three young people and the robot followed the detector's signal.

Tom looked up at the planet Jupiter, a gigantic disk filling the sky on all sides. He could see the Great Red Spot, that enormous atmospheric storm that had lasted for centuries. The expedition had hoped to discover new information about it. They would still go home knowing more than anyone had ever known before, but. . . .

"Watch out!" Anita yelled suddenly.

Tom and Ben instantly realized the danger Anita had sensed, but they were powerless to do anything about it!

It was too late!

Chapter Eight

Tom felt the rover dip out from under him and there was a sudden sensation of falling. They were going over the edge of one of the many sulci in the area!

As the vehicle slid over the rim of the big ice crevasse and started down the deep side, the young people held on tightly so they would not be thrown out of the rover and crushed, or puncture their suits. Tom was not as concerned about Aristotle since the robot was far less fragile than the humans.

They hit the bottom of the sulcus and the rover bounced hard three times before Tom was finally able to wrestle it under control.

"Is anyone hurt?" he asked anxiously, turning in his seat to look at his friends.

"I'm okay," said Ben.

"So am I," Anita confirmed.

Aristotle, who had gripped the sides of the rover with his hydraulic hands, had managed to stay in the vehicle, too. Tom checked the robot, and was greatly relieved that Aristotle had survived the rough trip without damage.

"Thank goodness for the weaker gravity up here," said Tom as he looked at the way they had come down. "If this had happened on Earth we would have been badly injured for sure."

"Hey!" Ben said excitedly. "The indicator light is blinking like crazy. We're very close!" The young man got out of the rover and turned slowly, watching the detector. "This way," he said, and started walking.

Tom looked around the bleak, icy surface. Why was there no sign of any wreckage?

"There should be parts and equipment scattered all over the crash site, but I don't see anything," he told Anita and Aristotle. "I guess we'll just have to follow Ben!"

When the rover caught up to him, Ben climbed back in. "How much air do we have with us?" he asked.

"Another two-hour container for each of us,"

said Tom. "But I have a little over twenty minutes in my present tank. How about you two?"

Anita and Ben had about the same amount of air.

"We should wait a bit before changing tanks," Anita said. "We can use the time to explore the area around here. Then, after we change tanks we can go farther off if we have to."

Breathing mixture was used to the very end of each tank in order to stretch the amount of time each person could stay away from the *Daniel Boone*. Changing tanks with more than a quarter hour of air left in them was considered wasteful except in emergency conditions.

"That's fine," said Ben, "because according to the detector, we're right on top of the wreckage. But I don't see a thing! We'll have to make a thorough search of the area!"

Tom looked around. The terrain seemed different from what they had been traveling over, but he could not figure out exactly what the difference was. It bothered him that he could not put his finger on it.

"Let's spread out," Tom advised, "but don't go out of sight of the rover."

The three young people loped off in different directions. The robot, as usual, stayed within visual range of Tom who picked his way carefully around the spiky ice formations that covered the area. There were many theories about the surface structure of Ganymede and they all involved high-pressure ice physics.

But the most baffling feature, to planetologists, had always been the type of formation the young people were now exploring, the sulci. The pattern of these mysterious grooves seemed to suggest that in Ganymede's past there had been considerable tectonic activity—twisting, sliding, and stretching of surface material. Yet something was missing. There was no evidence of new surface material, only a solid blanket of ice.

"Tom!" The young inventor recognized Anita's voice. "I think I've—" The rest of her sentence was drowned in a sudden explosion of static. Tom Swift hurriedly adjusted the reception on his radio, trying to find her signal again.

"Anita, I'm getting too much static," he said, hoping she could hear him. "There must be something wrong with your suit radio."

"What's going on?" Ben asked.

"Something happened, Tom," said Aristotle.

Tom turned in the direction Anita had taken, deploring the limited visibility and the sense-deadening qualities of the spacesuits.

The young woman was nowhere to be seen! She had disappeared from the surface entirely!

"Anita!" he called out again, trying to suppress the panic in his voice. He knew that to panic would be the worst thing any of them could do.

"Anita's circuits are patterned on my memory," Aristotle declared. Then he fell silent, but Tom knew that he was using every one of his sensors to locate the redhead.

Suddenly Ben leaped toward him. He was using the light gravity to cover distance quickly by bounding across the surface. "Where's Anita?" he asked anxiously.

"Slow down, Ben," said Tom. "If you fall, you'll tear your suit! We'll find her, don't worry."

But Tom was also worried about the girl. How could she have disappeared without a trace?

He kept yelling through the static on the radio, "Anita!" There was no answer.

Aristotle suddenly moved forward.

"My sonarscan indicates that the surface beyond me is not solid, Tom," he said. "We must look for signs of fresh breakage in the crust. I believe Anita may have fallen through."

Tom studied the surface of the sulcus again. Aristotle's theory made sense. The crust *was* different here. In fact, it looked as though, sometime in the ancient past, it had been subjected to tremendous heat, and then liquified. It had refrozen almost immediately, leaving meringue-like peaks over the area. Some parts could easily be weaker than others!

Aristotle stopped. He scanned the area with his cameras and then turned his sensorframe toward Tom. "The surface may not support my weight beyond this point, Tom."

Wait here, then," the young inventor instructed. "Ben, bring the rover over here so we can get the emergency cable and something to gig with."

"Right," said the young Indian, and hurried off. Tom walked forward, cautiously. He tested his weight on the surface before taking each step.

Suddenly, the icy crust broke beneath his cleated boot and he pitched onto his knees.

He had stumbled into an air-pocket formation. But there was no air on Ganymede! It was much too cold. Any atmospheric gasses would be frozen. But what if the theory about the surface formations were true? The sudden heat could have liberated the frozen gasses long enough for them to form pockets within the melted ice. When it all froze again, the atmospheric gasses would have flash-frozen too, but pockets would have remained, creating treacherous terrain.

Tom looked out over the barren expanse in

frustration. Was Anita hurt badly? Unconscious? And what about her air supply? She should have several minutes of air left—unless she had damaged her air tanks. Tom and Ben would be able to get the fresh tanks from the rover, but they would have to find Anita before her supply ran out!

Tom squinted hard, trying to spot any places where there might be a fresh disturbance on the surface. It was so dark. The shielded helmet visor tended to distort things a little, too. It was maddening.

Tom watched as Ben drove up and motioned to him.

"Stop there," the young inventor said to his friend. "We can't risk losing the rover."

"At least we can light the area," said Ben. "There are emergency work lights that run off batteries."

"We'll have to use them sparingly, though," Tom cautioned, getting a large roll of braided steel cable and a shovel out of the vehicle. "We have no way of recharging the batteries and we need the rover to get back to the base camp."

Ben nodded and began setting up the work lights.

Abruptly, Aristotle moved forward. Tom noticed that the robot was not traveling in a straight line. Instead, he was zigzagging along the moon's rough surface.

"Follow us with the work lights, Ben," said Tom, and began walking in the mechanoid's tracks.

"I am using my sonarscan to find the solid ground," the robot explained. "It will also tell me where the surface is weak. The last time I saw Anita, she was traveling in this direction."

Tom was glad he had the robot to be his eyes and ears on Ganymede. If an accident like this had happened on Earth, he would have heard the ground cave in under Anita, and his sight would not be so limited by the helmet of a spacesuit. Here, his senses were deadened by his survival equipment.

Aristotle stopped suddenly and stood in silence for a few seconds. Then he raised one arm and pointed to his right. Tom saw that the surface at that spot was slightly raised and bubble-like, but it was hard to tell anything else in the darkness.

"I am getting some unusual echoes from that formation, Tom," the robot stated. "There are solid metal objects beneath the crust—and Anita is there. I know her circuits."

The area was suddenly flooded with light. Ben

had been monitoring Tom's conversation with Aristotle and had aimed the work lights at the spot the robot had indicated. Now the ground looked even more barren and alien. Tom tried to see as far as he could into the distance. Was the surface broken? He just couldn't tell. The static coming over his suit radio only fed his frustration. Anita could be buried forever under tons of ice, or she could be trying to dig her way out of a deep crevasse. Tom had no way of knowing.

"How much do the objects you are carrying weigh, Tom?" asked the robot. "I must figure the extra weight into my calculations."

Tom hefted the cable. In the one-sixth gravity of Ganymede, there was really no way of telling exactly how much it weighed. "There's about a hundred feet of it," he replied. "On Earth, it would be about twenty pounds. Figure about seven more pounds for the shovel."

"You may proceed, Tom," said the robot. "Go to the left of your present position for approximately five paces, then make a ninety-degree turn to the right."

Tom did as the robot directed. He began to notice a definite upward slope.

"Stop," he heard Aristotle say, a few moments later. "I suggest you test the surface very carefully from here on."

Using the shovel as a probe, Tom examined the ground one step at a time. It was painfully slow. He stabbed the shovel into the ice, then took a step. Stabbed, then . . .

Suddenly, the ice gave way beneath him and he fell. It was a slow, tumbling kind of descent. He heard Ben's voice calling him anxiously all the way down.

"I am sorry, Tom," Aristotle said, then all was quiet.

Tom Swift opened his eyes and looked up. A spacesuited figure was bending over him. It was Anita! From his suit radio, he heard Ben's frantic shouts.

"Tom! Answer me, Tom!" the young Indian was yelling.

"Everything is fine, Ben," Tom replied. "I've found Anita. I think she's all right."

Tom could see the girl nodding her head. She pantomimed falling through the surface and then landing on her suit's transmitter. Then she made an "okay" sign with her gloved fingers, which meant she could hear the two boys and Aristotle. It must have been frustrating for Anita to know her friends were trying to rescue her and to be unable to help them, Tom thought.

He got up and put his arms around the girl in

an awkward spacesuit hug. He saw tears of relief rolling down her cheeks.

"I am pleased that you found Anita, and that both of you are all right," Aristotle said. "My errors caused these accidents. I would not blame you if you shut me down."

Anita looked at Tom with concern.

"Aristotle, will you *please* stop blaming yourself for everything that happens!" said Tom, exasperated. "There *are* such things as accidents, you know. I programed that bit of information into you, remember?"

"I am sorry," the robot apologized. Tom grimaced with annoyance. Some day he was going to have to deal with the mechanoid's inferiority complex.

Anita made a wide gesture with her arms indicating their surroundings. They had fallen into a huge underground cave! The sides were smooth, but the bottom was littered with rocks and chunks of ice—and pieces of equipment pod number four! That is why they had not seen any wreckage. From the ground, it had been impossible to detect the presence of the cave. Tom knew it must be at least a mile in diameter and hundreds of feet deep in some places. The whole area was probably covered with "bubble caves" of this kind.

"The pod's here," Tom said. "It looks all broken up. There's no way of knowing if any of the equipment is still usable until we get back to the base camp."

"Right," Ben replied. His voice had suddenly become tense. "Look, you'll both need air soon. My air level indicator just flipped over!"

Tom checked his own instrument, then looked at Anita. She nodded her head vigorously, confirming that hers, like Tom's, had already turned from green to orange.

That meant they had less than seven minutes of air left!

A shiver ran down Tom's spine. Would they be able to get a new supply before their time ran out?

Chapter Nine

Tom knew that they could only survive if Ben was able to lower new air tanks into the cave.

"There's some cable in the rover," he said to his friend, "but it's not enough. I have most of it down here, so I'll have to throw it to you."

He looked around the bottom of the cave for something with which to weight the end of the cable. From the equipment pod wreckage he selected a heavy piece of twisted framework.

Quickly he unwrapped the cable and wound one end around the metal. Anita watched him anxiously, hoping the cable would be long enough. She knew the fragile air tanks could not be dropped, or they would break!

103

When Tom had tied the metal securely, he called to Ben. "I'm going to toss it out now. I just hope I can throw it high enough to clear the walls."

He spun the end of the cable using the weight of the metal to build up momentum. Then he threw it into the air with all his strength. He and Anita watched it sail slowly upward, then fall back toward them. It had risen just short of the opening at the top of the ice cave.

"No go, Ben," said Tom. "I'll try again." This time, the young inventor jumped into the air as high as he could before flinging his arm back for the toss. It threw him off balance, but the cable sailed over the rim of the cave.

"Got it!" Ben exclaimed, relieved, and Anita jumped up and down excitedly.

She and Tom watched as the cable was being drawn up through the hole.

Soon an air tank was snaking down toward them. The two young people stepped back to avoid being hit by pieces of ice broken off by the cable.

"Easy, Ben," said Tom, as the tank neared the bottom. As soon as he could reach it, the young man quickly untied the tank. He took it over to Anita and exchanged it for her empty one, which he fastened to the cable. "Pull it up, Ben," he called out over his suit's radio. Even though the tank was empty, it was valuable. At the base camp, it would be refilled and used again. A few seconds later, Ben lowered a second tank.

Just as Tom reached for it, the indicator in his suit flipped from orange to red! He was out of air except for the little amount in his suit!

Quickly he replaced the used tank with the fresh one, taking a great gulp of air when the process was completed. That had been much too close for comfort!

The young man motioned to Anita and the two of them looked at the scattered pieces of the equipment pod.

"We'll have to get as much of this stuff back to the base camp as possible," he told the redhead. She nodded, and together they went to work. First they picked out any piece of equipment that appeared valuable, then they tied each item to the end of the cable for Ben to pull up. Soon the job was done, and Tom asked Ben to rescue Anita and himself.

"Okay," said Ben. "I'm glad you're done because we have just about enough air left to get us back to the base camp."

Tom motioned for Anita to go first. She was reluctant, but he insisted and she finally gave in. Tom tied the cable securely around her, making sure that it would not interfere with any of her life-support systems.

"Take her up carefully," Tom urged Ben. Then he added, "Aristotle, help him, will you please?"

Tom watched Anita's ascent. When she had safely disappeared over the lip of the hole, he suddenly had an idea. He went back to the wreckage and fished through it until he found something he had seen earlier. It was the twisted mass of the pod's electronic components. If he had the physical evidence, maybe he could prove to Aristotle that the pod's crash had not been the robot's fault. He knew he had to do something, or Aristotle's self-confidence would continue to deteriorate!

Tom shook his head slowly. Who ever would have thought that a machine could develop an inferiority complex? Yet Aristotle was certainly beginning to exhibit just such a human trait!

Tom had no idea how the robot had acquired the human tendencies. None of the other mechanoids came close to showing any kind of emotions or feelings. Of course, none of them were as sophisticated as Aristotle, either. Not by a long shot, he thought proudly. There must be something in the extra programing and sensitivity that Tom had given his mechanoid that had prompted these human characteristics to develop in him.

Whatever it was, Tom was going to have a problem on his hands if he did not deal with it soon!

Once they were safely back on the *Daniel Boone,* the news of their discovery spread like wildfire.

"Those ice caves were a great find, Tom" the young inventor heard someone say from behind him. He flipped himself around, using one of the stabilizing bars hooked to the bulkhead, and saw Dr. Sung Vangumtorn waving at him from the ship's main elevator. The Thai planetologist and his team were on their way to the base camp with the last of their equipment, and Tom knew they had already planned a trip to the ice caves.

Tom grinned. "When you get there, don't fall in like we did, though!"

"I'll be smarter than that!" the scientist teased as the elevator door closed.

Tom floated toward the lab door and looked down the long deserted corridor of the ship. Now that they were in geosynchronous orbit around Ganymede, the spin had been taken off the ship. There were not many people left aboard, apart from the navy crew, and they had to adjust to the weightless condition.

Since the Ganymede base was close to comple-
tion, everyone, except for the personnel necessary to maintain the big interplanetary ship, had
moved there. Everyone except the Friedmans.

Most of the construction material for their
dome, and almost all of their instruments had
been destroyed in the crash of their equipment
pod. Even though the young people were doing
their best to help the astronomers examine the
wreckage they had salvaged, they had found very
little that could be of use. Tom knew the Friedmans felt like dead weight to the rest of the expedition, and he wished there was something he
could do to make the trip worthwhile to them despite their misfortunes.

He floated through the hatch of the lab, and to
his surprise, saw his friends and Aristotle gathered around Ian Friedman. There was something
bolted down on the work table in front of the
young astronomer.

Anita looked up and motioned to Tom excitedly. "See what Ian put together last night," she
said.

As Tom floated toward the group, he noticed
that Ian must have gone without sleep for quite
some time. The young scientist looked pale and
worn, and there were dark circles under his eyes.

But he was smiling proudly. On the work table

in front of him lay the capsule belonging to one of the probes that the Friedmans had been planning to send to various other moons of Jupiter. Data from the cameras on those probes, plus results of the core samples that the devices were to have taken, would have composed much of the team's research. Somehow, Ian had been able to rebuild one probe from the pieces of the other six.

"I don't know what good it will do," the young astronomer said. "There is no way to send it anywhere. This is just the instrument package. The propulsion part of it was destroyed. But I—I just had to do something!"

Tom looked at the probe, then stared out the window into space for a moment. "Which probe was this?" he asked.

"Most of it is the Io instrument package," Ian replied, "but there are parts of the Callisto and the Amalthea packages here, too."

"Do you think it will still function on Io?" asked Tom.

"I don't know. There's not as much heat-shielding on it now as there was on the original probe. It doesn't matter, though. The thing's not going anywhere!"

Ben noticed a mysterious smile on Tom's face. "You've got an idea, haven't you?" he asked his friend. "I can just hear those gears meshing in your brain."

Ian was puzzled. "What's going on?"

Tom's smile grew. "When I come back, I want you guys to have some ideas for heat-shielding for the probe," he declared. "That means you, too, Aristotle! I've got to go check with a man about borrowing a ship!"

Without another word, Tom left the lab and headed for the elevator. "Bridge," he said to the computer as he pulled himself inside.

A few seconds later, he floated out onto the bridge. Two bored-looking young crew members with the words SHIP PATROL on their jumpsuits blocked his path.

"Identify yourself and state your business," one of the SPs said formally.

"I am Tom Swift and I am here to speak to Captain Barrot," replied Tom.

One of the SPs pushed off and floated toward a hatch that said NAVIGATION—AUTHORIZED PERSONNEL ONLY on it. He knocked and said, "Tom Swift requests permission to see the captain."

The hatch opened and Rafe Barrot stuck his head out. "Permission granted." He smiled at Tom, "Come on in!"

Tom pulled himself toward the hatch. "Thank you," he said as he passed the SP.

"It sure has been peaceful up here without all you civilians," Barrot teased him as he pulled himself into a seat beside the captain and buckled himself in to keep from accidentally floating into the sensitive equipment in the tiny room. There were switches, buttons, and digital readouts everywhere. Tom looked out of the viewport and saw the surface of Ganymede framed by the planet Jupiter. It still thrilled him.

"How's it going?" he asked. He didn't want to come right out with a request for the lander craft. Besides, it had been a long time since he had seen Rafe Barrot, whom he liked and respected very much.

"To tell you the truth, I'm bored stiff," Barrot replied, laughing. "It takes very little effort to maintain orbit and the regular navy guys are driving me crazy with all their spit and polish ways! I would rather be down on the surface where all the action is. But a captain belongs on his ship, so here I sit!"

Tom nodded sympathetically. He knew that Barrot was the rugged, adventuresome type; the kind of person who did not thrive under the burden of routine. The young inventor was counting on that spirit to aid him in his request.

"What brings you up here, Tom?" Barrot asked.

"I need a ship," Tom replied.

Barrot sat back in his chair and smiled. Tom could tell he had sparked the captain's curiosity.

"Why do you need a ship?"

"I want to plant an instrument package on Io and find out what happened to the Argus probe."

"You want one of the long-range landing craft, then. Who did you plan to take with you?"

"Ben Walking Eagle, Anita Thorwald, and Aristotle, my robot."

"I can't put you in charge of a navy vessel, Tom. An officer of the U. S. Navy would have to pilot the ship."

"I understand, sir. But does that mean you are granting my request?"

"Maybe." Barrot paused for a moment, obviously deep in thought. "What you are proposing to do is very dangerous, although it is something that pertains to the success of the Jupiter exploratory mission. It would certainly help the astronomy team and right now they need every bit of help they can get." Barrot paused briefly, then went on.

"Your father is my friend, Tom. I have worked with him through the years and grown to respect his judgment without reservation. I would feel better if you had his permission. Have you talked with him about this yet?"

"No, sir. I came right to you."

"If he says it is okay, they I don't see any reason why I shouldn't let you have a ship. You have more experience in space than most of the people here and I know you can handle yourself in emergency situations. Let me see who's on the duty roster."

Barrot swiveled in his chair and faced a small CRT. He punched out a code on the miniature terminal and a list of names appeared. The last one was blinking. "Lieutenant Junior Grade Burt Foster is your man," said the captain, smiling. "He's navy all the way through, so he'll expect a lot of formality from you." The older man's expression grew wistful. "I sure do wish I could go with you!"

"I don't know how to thank you, sir," said Tom.

"You still have to ask your father's permission," Barrot reminded him. "Unless he approves, you don't get the ship."

Tom shook hands with the captain and left the bridge. Instead of going back to the lab, he got his spacesuit and sent a message to his father that he would be coming to see him. Then he went straight to the shuttle bay and took the first ship bound for the Ganymede base. His father was waiting for him when he arrived.

"Well, Tom," said the elder Swift. "I'm very anxious to know what is so important that it couldn't wait until the end of the work cycle!"

Father and son loped slowly across the short distance from the landing area to the airlock of the main dome. The elder Swift cycled the lock and then, after a few seconds, they stepped from there into the decontamination shower.

As the liquid carried away the last traces of Jupiter's radiation, Tom organized his thoughts. He hated to give a "hard sell" to his own father, but getting this ship was important to him and, besides, it could mean everything for the Friedmans.

"Come with me," said Mr. Swift when they had finished removing their suits.

The interior of the main dome was a marvel. Every time Tom visited it, the work crew and the residents had added improvements for making it as comfortable as possible.

The dome had been divided into sections for living quarters, lab facilities, and common rooms. This had been done by erecting framework panels and spraying them with dome foam.

The same principle had been used as a base for building the upper levels.

The main floor was actually below ground and had been finished first. The "human touch" had been added by the use of paint in warm colors. Tom could see that the geometric design motif was spreading to the level above, too.

The elder Swift entered a cubicle and motioned for his son to follow.

"These are my living quarters now. Make yourself at home."

Tom had to admit that his father's cubicle was very cozy. He wondered if the others were similar to it.

"I don't want to take up too much of your time, Dad," said Tom. "I know how busy you are. I just want your permission to take a ship to Io."

Tom's father looked at him, surprised. "May I ask why you want to go to Io?" he asked, his voice full of concern.

"Ian Friedman was able to salvage one of the instrument packages from pod number four, but he has no way to plant it. I want to see the Friedmans come out of this expedition with something, Dad, and besides, you know we've been wondering what exactly happened to the Argus probe. If I can find it, maybe I can fix it."

Quickly the young inventor told his father about the conversation with Captain Barrot.

"You make it sound so simple," said the elder Swift, "but have you thought of the incredible danger involved? No man has ever been to Io before. In addition to all the known hazards, there could be problems we are not even aware of. Since the Argus probe is not functioning correctly, it has not been able to supply us with the information we need before even considering a manned expedition."

Mr. Swift studied his son carefully. His expression was worried. "Tom, you don't know what you are getting into. I cannot overemphasize the possible hazards involved."

"Yes, but I've done dangerous things before, and you've never tried to stop me."

Mr. Swift could not keep back a chuckle. "I don't think I could. You're too much like me. It's not easy for me to see you go, though. You're my only son and I love you very much."

Tom swallowed hard. He knew what his father must be feeling. It would never be easy for him to see his son going out on a dangerous mission, from which he might not return.

"You have good instincts, Tom," his father went on, "and you know how to handle yourself in a crisis. Do you really think this trip is necessary?"

"Yes, Dad, I do."

"Then I'll radio my permission to Rafe. Just be careful, Son."

"I will, Dad. And, thanks!"

"Good luck, Tom."

Chapter Ten

The officer in charge of the *Daniel Boone's* shuttle bay regarded Tom, Anita, Ben, and the robot critically. Then he looked at the CRT of his computerized activities roster. "You've been assigned to the *Meriwether Lewis* with Lieutenant Foster in command," he said. "She's on launch deck number two. Try to bring her back in one piece!"

"Uh—we sure will," said Tom, and walked quickly past the man.

"He doesn't approve of our mission," Anita declared when they were out of the officer's hearing range. "It's because he doesn't trust us, even with a fellow naval officer along."

"You may be right," Tom agreed.

"I *know* I'm right. That's the trouble with being an empath."

"A what?" asked Ben.

"A human being with the ability to read and share another being's emotions," Aristotle explained.

"Aristotle has been helping me do some research on the subject," said the beautiful redhead, smiling at the robot affectionately.

"Aristotle has been *helping* you?" asked Tom.

Anita nodded. "I asked him not to say anything until I told you," she said. "I was afraid you might think I was crazy. I wanted some proof that empaths really exist."

"It was not a violation of my prime directive not to mention it, Tom," said Aristotle. "Had you asked me, I would have had to tell Anita's secret. Since you did not ask—"

"I know," Tom laughed. "I didn't ask you and therefore you didn't *have* to bring it up!"

"Anita and I have shared current, you know," said the robot. "She is my friend."

"That makes you 'circuit brothers,'" Ben teased.

"What?" asked Anita.

"There's a custom among some Indian tribes for friends to cut their fingers and let their blood mingle. The belief is that they'll be friends for life—'blood brothers,' it is called."

Anita laughed. "When Mister Swift told me that the new micro-computer chip was influencing my nervous system, I became more aware of how it was affecting me. Now that I understand more of those strange feelings I've been having, I can control them a little and sometimes even use them to my advantage."

"That's how you were able to tell that the duty officer doesn't trust us?" asked Ben. "I bet all of the navy people think we're going to wreck their ship and kill ourselves on this trip!"

Anita nodded. "Not all of them, but some of them, yes."

"No civilians are permitted in this area without clearance. Identify yourselves immediately," a harsh voice said from behind them.

Tom whirled around, angry at being challenged so rudely. A young naval officer, carrying a duffel bag, walked stiffly up to them.

"I said—"

"Just who are *you?*" Tom asked.

"It doesn't work that way, Mister," replied the officer sharply. "Now, before I call the SPs, just who are you and why are you leading this freak parade through restricted access sections of a naval vessel?"

"I'm Tom Swift and this is *not* a freak parade! My friends and I are duly authorized to be here!" Tom showed the young man their passes. "We're going with the *Meriwether Lewis* on an exploratory mission to Io. We are the crew. Now," he asked again, "who are you?"

"Oh, no!" the officer said. "Nobody told me about this. I'm not going anywhere with *this* crew!" He glared at them for a moment, then brushed rudely past and burst through the double doors marked LAUNCH DECK 2.

"I think that was Lieutenant Junior Grade Burt Foster," Tom declared.

"He's going to be one great traveling companion," Ben added sarcastically.

"He scares me," Anita said. Tom could tell she was worried. "I don't understand why you can't pilot the ship, Tom!"

"The *Meriwether Lewis* is officially a naval vessel, although Swift Enterprises designed and built her. I'm not in the navy, so I'm not allowed to pilot their ships. We can't go without Lieutenant Foster, so we had better learn to get along with him the best we can!"

"I am with you, Tom," said Aristotle. The robot's remark surprised and amused everyone. They continued to joke with Aristotle as they passed through the doors of the launch deck, but their laughter died when they saw the sullen, resentful look on the young lieutenant's face as he watched them approach the ship.

Tom walked up to him smiling, even though Foster stared at him with undisguised hostility.

"I think we got off to a bad start," the young inventor said, trying not to make his friendliness look like an effort. "Let's put our personal differences aside for the good of this mission, okay?"

"Our differences are *not* personal, Mister Swift," said Foster coolly. "They are purely professional. Any time a mere civilian can—" Abruptly, he clicked his heels together and saluted. Tom turned to see Rafe Barrot walking toward them.

The captain was smiling but there was an obvious tension behind his friendly expression. Did it have something to do with Foster's complaints about the civilians? Tom felt sure that Foster had talked to a superior officer after their first encounter.

Was it possible the story had traveled to Barrot's ear so quickly? It was almost unheard of for the captain of a ship like the *Daniel Boone* to personally send off a tiny expedition like this one— unless he thought something might be wrong.

Barrot returned Foster's salute. "At ease, Lieutenant," he said. Foster shifted to the proper military stance with crisp precision. He was, however, far from being "at ease." Tom was not sure, but he suspected that Rafe Barrot had noticed it, too.

"I wanted to see that you got off to a good start," Captain Barrot said to the civilians. Then he turned to the junior officer.

"You know, you're not flying this ship all by yourself, Lieutenant Foster. Tom Swift has logged a lot of time in space and he's an excellent pilot. He will be a big help to you. I want you to listen to him if he has any suggestions."

"Yes, sir," Foster said. Tom was sure that the young naval officer was perceptive enough to realize that he had been given an order. It had been tactfully phrased to save him from embarrassment because of his earlier protests, but it was an order, nevertheless.

The captain left, and the crew settled into their positions aboard the lander craft. Anita, Ben, and Aristotle took their places in the section behind the bridge. Tom sat in the copilot's couch and began the copilot's pre-takeoff routine.

The unpleasant scene with Lieutenant Foster continued to trouble him. Was it possible the young man's hostility was simply based on the fact they were civilians? Or was there something else causing it as well?

"Just what do you think you are doing?" a harsh voice asked from the doorway.

Tom turned to Lieutenant Foster and, with great effort, replied calmly. "I am fulfilling my responsibilities as copilot by making the necessary manual checks." He continued to meet the lieutenant's eye as he added, "Would you rather I do something else first?"

"Who said you were copilot?" Foster demanded.

"Captain Barrot just suggested that I should help you since I have logged a lot of time in space. This ship needs a copilot so I assumed—"

"That is correct," the naval officer snapped as he moved to the pilot's couch. "You assumed."

He whirled to Tom in anger. "You are *not* to assume. *I* am the captain of this ship, not you. Is that *clearly* understood? I do not care who your father is, or how well you know Captain Barrot, or how famous you are back on Earth. On this ship you are just a mere crew member and you are *never* to assume any responsibility unless I— repeat—*I* delegate it to you."

His voice became almost terrifyingly cold. "Is that *perfectly* clear, Mister Swift?"

Tom was dumbfounded. So that was why Lieutenant Foster had been so angry. He was jealous of Tom and his father and their relationship with his commanding officer!

The Swifts had become accustomed to the fact that some people would always be jealous of them. It was unfortunate, but there were those who did not see all the hard work and the sweat which went into the inventions coming out of Swift Enterprises. Those people saw only the publicity and acclaim which resulted.

It made Tom sad when he ran into this self-defeating attitude. He could not understand why people would expend so much energy in hate and envy when they could be doing something worthwhile, bringing pleasure to themselves as well as others.

Now that he understood a little why Lieutenant Foster's behavior was so hostile, he had a better chance of not provoking him.

"Yes, Lieutenant," Tom replied quietly, in as correct a military manner as possible. "Your orders are perfectly clear, sir."

The young officer seemed to relax somewhat. "Then I hereby appoint you temporary copilot of this ship until further notice. Begin at once to undertake preflight manual checks. We are running late," Foster snapped.

Tom resisted the strong impulse to point out

that he had been doing exactly that when Foster himself had interrupted him. He just hoped that this important trip would not be jeopardized by the stubborn, hostile behavior of the lieutenant.

The *Meriwether Lewis* had just passed the lightly orange-hued moon, Europa, the second closest of the Galilean moons to Jupiter, when Aristotle moved up behind Tom. "Will you please come with me to check the cargo hold?" the robot asked.

Tom swiveled around in surprise, then nodded. He unbuckled his restraining harness and floated free of the form-fitting couch.

"Permission to check the equipment package," requested Tom, going along with the formality Foster had required of his "crew."

Foster, sitting next to Tom in the pilot's couch, did not even look up. He seemed to be absorbed with the navigational instruments. "Permission granted," he finally mumbled.

Tom left the bridge with a sigh of relief. He kept pace with the robot by pulling himself along on the handholds built into the ship, since the *Meriwether Lewis* did not produce artificial gravity, as did the *Daniel Boone*. Aristotle was using his motorframe as an electromagnet to keep from floating.

Tom waved a greeting to Ben and Anita as he and the robot passed them in the corridor that separated the bridge from the rest of the ship. Normally, they would have stopped to chat about the expedition and plans for exploring the surface of Io, but Foster's attitude discouraged conversation.

Anita smiled rather nervously at Tom as she passed. The young inventor could almost sense the tension that Foster had created on the ship. He was sure Anita was feeling it more strongly than any of them. He decided it would serve no useful purpose to tell his friends about his confrontation with the young officer.

"Why don't you shut down for a while?" he said, gently putting a hand on Anita's shoulder as she floated near him. "You don't need to walk in zero G and with your computer off, you won't be so sensitive to everything that's going on."

"That's a good idea," said Anita, emotional fatigue in her voice.

"I'll help you," Ben said to her. Then the young computer tech turned to Tom and Aristotle. "Is something up?" he asked.

"No," Tom answered casually. "We're just going to check the cargo. I wanted to stretch my legs a little, anyway. I've been on the couch for hours and when we get close to Io, I'm going to have to be on it again for quite a while."

He paused, then added, "When you get back to the bridge, Ben, would you run a check on the computer-controlled exterior cameras? I promised the Friedmans that we'd get some good close-ups of Jupiter as well as Io."

"Sure," said Ben, "but hurry back, will you? It's awful being on the bridge with just Foster!" With that, he and Anita continued along the narrow corridor.

Tom looked after them for a moment. He had wanted to tell them that yes, something was up, but it wouldn't do any good to alarm them before he talked with Aristotle. The robot was disturbed, Tom knew that for sure, because Aristotle was perfectly capable of checking the cargo himself.

They entered the cargo room and Tom shut and locked the hatch behind them. "Okay, what's wrong?" he asked the robot.

"I have been communicating with the navigation section of the ship's computer, Tom. It is a relatively low-order intelligence, but sometimes I just need to talk with another machine. I hope you understand. Anyway, I was curious about our course, so I asked for details. Have you checked Lieutenant Foster's calculations?"

"No," replied Tom. "I've tried to ask questions and make suggestions to him, but every time I do, he acts as though I am plotting mutiny! He's very suspicious of me and won't tell me anything. What did you find out?"

"We are in grave danger!"

Chapter Eleven

Tom stared at Aristotle in surprise. "What do you mean?"

"Lieutenant Foster has plotted a course to Io that will bring us quite close to Jupiter—in my estimation, too close. We need an immediate course correction to keep us well away from Jupiter and its immense gravitational pull. Otherwise we will be drawn into the planet and crushed."

"We are going tangential to Jupiter? Like someone cutting across a lawn to get to the sidewalk?"

"Checking." There was a slight pause. "Yes, I believe that illustration is essentially correct. It is my opinion the Lieutenant Foster is not a sufficiently expert pilot to complete the course without danger."

"Oh, boy—"

"In addition, his plotted course indicates an attempted landing on Io without taking the precaution of orbiting the moon to insure the necessary deceleration for landing or identifying a proper landing site.

"In short, he's trying to prove he's a hot-shot pilot by throwing out every safety precaution in the book!" Tom stormed. "I wonder if he even knows whether the *Meriwether Lewis* is capable of that kind of maneuvering?"

Tom had been watching Foster handle the supple short-range scout ship with little respect and a heavy hand so far, and had been disheartened. Now, it actually frightened him.

"From the records I have been able to check, it would appear the officer's knowledge of this class of ship has been limited to routine training and shuttle flights. At no time has he flown it under the conditions it will be experiencing during the course as presently set," Aristotle said.

"He has to be stopped," Tom said slowly. "But how?"

"You must do something soon," Aristotle agreed.

"I guess this is where I test whether or not the lieutenant will follow Rafe Barrot's advice about listening to me."

"I predict he will not, but you must try," the robot said.

"How was the cargo?" Foster asked when Tom and Aristotle came back to the bridge.

Tom pulled himself into his couch and connected the restraining harness. "The equipment package is riding fine," he replied. Then, as casually as he possibly could, he added, "You've been working awfully hard ever since we started. Why don't you take a short break and let me run the ship for a while, Lieutenant?"

Instantly he saw anger flare up in Foster's eyes.

"That won't be necessary," the officer said coldly.

Tom decided to try another approach. "Have you run a computer simulation of our course yet? Maybe we should do that." Such a procedure would give Foster a chance to change his mind if he wanted to and to correct his calculations without being directly challenged by Tom.

"Let me worry about that," the lieutenant snapped. It was obvious that Foster had taken the comment as a challenge. Subtlety was just not going to work, Tom thought sadly. He had hoped he would not have to risk an open confrontation by questioning the officer's plans, but there seemed to be no other way to check the figures.

"All right, Lieutenant," said Tom reluctantly. "Aristotle thinks your course is very risky. I trust him and I want to know what you're trying to prove by endangering all of us!"

Behind him, Ben and Anita gasped aloud.

To his amazement, Foster leaned back on his couch and smiled. "I'm not endangering us. I'm saving a lot of time, that's all. Why don't you civilians just relax and do a little sightseeing? Leave the piloting to a real pro like me." He chuckled as he turned back to his instruments.

"If I do that, we might be killed!" Tom exploded angrily. "Why won't you listen to reason? You're so eaten up with jealousy that you're willing to sacrifice our lives to prove you're a better pilot than I am. That's *stupid!*"

Foster's smile disappeared. "I won't tolerate insubordination on my ship, Mister Swift!" he warned.

"You were ordered to let me help you, but you have insisted on running the whole show yourself. That was fine with me until now. Now you're about to kill us all. I will not let you do it! As co-pilot, I demand my right to check those figures!"

"Consider yourself under arrest, Swift!" the officer said coldly.

"You're crazy, Foster!" the young man protested.

"You bet I'm crazy—crazy for accepting an assignment to play galactic chauffeur for a bunch of civilians and their pet tin man. I'm the laughingstock of the entire *Daniel Boone!*"

"Only in your mind, Lieutenant," said Tom, trying to reason with the young man. "I know that some of the officers aboard the *Daniel Boone* think that the navy people are too good to associate with the civilians, but you forget one important fact—civilians designed and built these navy ships you're so proud of!"

"Gentlemen," interrupted Aristotle, "I strongly suggest that you correct your course now and settle your disagreement later."

The sharpness of the robot's tone caused chills to run up and down Tom's spine. The bands of color that made up the only visible surface of Jupiter were losing their definition. There was no longer a sharp dividing line between them. One band seemed to flow into another, taking on the characteristics of swirling air currents.

"The course stands as plotted," Foster insisted.

"This is insane," shouted Anita. "Tom, stop him! Can't you take over the ship or something? He's—he's out of his mind!"

"If one of you makes a move to do that, I'll kill you! Under the circumstances, it is my right as captain of this vessel to maintain order under force of arms if necessary. To do that I will not hesitate to shoot any—or all—of you!"

No one moved.

"*Meriwether Lewis,* this is the *Daniel Boone.* Come in, *Meriwether Lewis.* Are you in distress?"

Foster jumped at the sound of the radio as if he had been stung. It was apparent to Tom that the lieutenant had forgotten everything except his hatred for everyone on board the ship.

But someone was keeping tabs on them.

Rafe Barrot?

Foster lunged at the radio. "We are beginning the final phase of our approach to Io. We are not in distress. Repeat. We are not in distress."

"*Meriwether Lewis,* we are tracking your present course and it is not—"

"*Meriwether Lewis* cutting transmission now," Foster snapped. Tom saw a flash of fear on his face for the first time. "We will resume communication when the Io landing is completed." Before the *Daniel Boone* could answer, Foster switched off the radio.

He turned back to Tom with a forced smile on his lips. "There's something else I've been meaning to tell you, Mister Oh-So-Important. When they held that Three-Corner Race that you won, I had just been assigned to the *Daniel Boone* in preparation for the Jupiter expedition. The navy wouldn't give me the leave of absence I needed to enter the competition. Now you're going to see who would have won, Mister Swift! . . . All hands, to your stations! Prepare for Jupiter flyby!"

"Foster," Tom said in a tight voice, "you're going to take us in too close! The gravitational pull is too much!"

"Afraid, Swift?" Foster sneered.

"Only crazy people aren't afraid," Tom said quietly, but he knew at once by the lieutenant's sharp look that his remark had been a terrible error.

The officer's fingers stabbed at the settings, changing the course still more, to direct the fast little ship even closer to the immense planet.

"No way!" shouted Ben suddenly, launching himself at Foster. His arms were outstretched, aiming for the lieutenant's throat. In the zero gravity, he literally flew across the bridge.

"Don't do that, Ben!" Tom yelled. The young inventor jumped into the air and used his body to block Ben's attack.

Ben did a backflip and spun away from Tom. "Why did you stop me?" he asked angrily, as he grasped a bulkhead handhold. He turned his body expertly, just as Tom had seen him do dozens of times in their games of null-gravity handball, and prepared to launch himself at Foster again.

"I stopped you because mutiny is still a crime punishable by death!" Tom snapped. "We may be civilians, but we're under naval orders."

"But the only alternative is to let this jerk run the ship right into Jupiter!"

Lieutenant Foster drew a laser pistol from a compartment inside his couch. "You've been given your orders," he shouted. "Snap to it!"

"All right," said the young computer tech. "We'll do it your way!" He floated over to a seat beside Anita and strapped himself in.

All at once, Tom realized that Anita did not seem to be nearly as upset by the critical situation as either Ben or he seemed to be. In fact, she had said nothing since she urged him to take over the ship earlier.

Neither had Aristotle.

Both of them seemed to be concentrating very

intently on something, but Tom could not figure out what it was.

"I could be in error, Tom," Aristotle said. "I am a flawed mechanism."

Was it Tom's imagination, or was Aristotle trying to give him a significant look?

Despite the filtering compound in the glassite viewport, the light in the bridge began to take on an orange tint that deepened rapidly as they approached the Great Red Spot of Jupiter, the largest single storm in the entire solar system. While there was no real movement in the Great Red Spot as a whole, they could see wisps of curling storms within it. Each of these "minor" storms was almost as large as the Earth itself. The pitlike swirl in the thick, banded atmosphere of the great planet was an awesome sight.

Tom tore his eyes from the hypnotic view and turned to Lieutenant Foster. The tense young officer's fingers were busy, moving over the blinking controls of the ship. Beads of perspiration glistened on his forehead.

"Use the attitude engines," Tom said harshly. "Give it every bit of speed you can—*get us out of here!*"

"Shut up!" Foster yelled, but Tom noticed that one hand went toward the controls of the liquid-fuel engines that served as the main guidance system for the *Meriwether Lewis*. Tom could tell that Foster was a man torn in half by his emotions. Part of him wanted to be practical and cautious, and part of him wanted to prove his superiority. Soon, it would be too late for it to matter which half won.

Foster fired the starboard attitude engines. The Great Red Spot shifted, slightly.

"Give it everything we have!" Tom said, making no attempt to hide the urgency in his voice. The view out of the ports had become hazy, as if they were entering a great orange cloud. They had actually penetrated the atmosphere of Jupiter!

Tom looked at the radar screens, but they showed very little. At least we aren't going to run into any air traffic out here, he thought.

The cloud thickened into an orange fog and almost simultaneously the ship began to quiver. The shivers became bucks as it fought the gravity and the turbulence of the Great Red Spot's eternal storms. The vessel twisted back and forth, then rolled hard to starboard.

Foster snarled as he attempted to bring the ship under control. Tom realized the lieutenant had become disoriented in his rage. He had fired the wrong attitude jets, pushing the ship farther inward instead of outward. The *Meriwether Lewis* screamed as the tortured metal was bent. It was like being on a runaway roller coaster.

"We're going right through the Great Red Spot!" Anita cried. "The gigantic storm will tear us apart!"

"Let me help you," Tom yelled at Foster. "You can't handle this by yourself anymore!"

"Not on your life!" Foster screamed back. "If you can't take it, that's just too bad!"

Tom grabbed for the vital controls of the ship. Foster hit him hard in the jaw. The boy was stunned by the blow, and shook his head to fend off the pain and dizziness.

Then, two metal arms wrapped themselves around Lieutenant Foster, pinning his arms. Foster yelled and struggled fiercely to break free, but human flesh was no match for hydraulic metal.

"*Aristotle!*" shouted Tom.

"There is no legal precedent for courtmartialing a robot, Tom. You must take control of the ship if we are to survive."

"You'll all die for this!" yelled Foster. "I'll see that you do! Let me go!"

Tom grasped the controls anxiously. Could he pull the *Meriwether Lewis* out of the grip of Jupiter in time? A thick slush that Tom knew had to be liquid hydrogen was already sticking to the glassite ports as they sped deeper and deeper into the atmosphere of the giant planet!

Chapter Twelve

Tom closed everything out of his mind except running the ship. He had trained himself long ago to achieve total concentration at will. He knew that he needed it now. There was no time for computerized course corrections or proper procedure.

The *Meriwether Lewis* had to become part of him—an extension of his body.

It was their only hope!

He felt the motions of the tortured ship as it fought not only the incredible gravity of Jupiter—three times that of Earth—but also the ripping, tearing winds which were swirling about them at hurricane strength. Luckily, this craft had been designed to endure high-stress situations. But no one had ever tested these conditions before. Could the little ship continue to survive them?

Tom pushed forward the fusion engine accelerator and at the same time gave the attitude engines full thrust away from Jupiter. He risked a quick look at the fuel gauge for the attitude engines: alarmingly low! The ship might lose the capability of finely tuned flying later, but if he did not make this effort now, there would *be* no later to deal with!

Behind him Ben and Anita sat, strapped in their places. Their bodies were rigid with the tension, every muscle trying to urge the ship to respond just a little faster. Their eyes were riveted to Tom's hands as he coaxed every possible ounce of power from the straining engines.

Outside, the atmosphere had thickened to burnt-orange slush. How deep was the atmosphere of Jupiter? Whatever it was, Tom had no desire to find out firsthand! He was flying "by the seat of his pants," by that set of senses which all natural pilots are born with. He knew that Jupiter was in one direction and escape was in another.

The build-up of the G-forces was beginning to tear at the fabric of the ship and its passengers. It took all of Tom's strength to keep his hands on the trembling controls, and he felt as if his skull was being crushed by a terrible, invisible weight.

He fought the dizziness that threatened his consciousness. If he blacked out now, the ship would go out of control and be lost forever.

The G-forces pushed him hard into the couch and he could hear Ben, Anita, and even Foster groan. It felt as if the air was being pressed out of their lungs and the blood was draining from their brains. Tom saw spots of fuzzy blackness in front of his eyes and his awareness seemed to blur.

But then there was a gradual lessening of the pressure. . . .

The ship still tossed about like a twig on a stormy sea, but Tom knew that they had beaten the gravitational force of Jupiter!

He and his friends were still breathing hard when he heard Foster growl, "You think you're so smart, Tom Swift! If we get out of here alive, I'll—" A choked noise of frustrated anger finished the sentence.

The orange soup became fog, then quickly thinned. They could see the stars once again!

"Ben, contact the *Daniel Boone* and outline our situation. It won't do much good, but they should know what's going on here," said Tom, ignoring Foster's threats.

"With pleasure," beamed Ben.

"What are you going to tell them?" shouted Foster. "Probably a bunch of lies! They'll never believe you. They'll know you took over the ship by force! When we get back to the *Daniel Boone,* I'm going to file a full report and press charges!" Foster twisted his head around until he could see Aristotle. "And I'm going to see that this hunk of metal is permanently shut down, too!"

"Sticks and stones will break my bones, but words will never hurt me!" the robot said laconically. Foster looked at him with pure hatred.

"Where did you learn *that?*" asked Tom, amazed. "I didn't program any colloquialisms into your memory!"

"I try to keep an open sensorframe and absorb all the knowledge about humans that I can," answered Aristotle.

The radio speaker crackled with static for a few seconds. "This is the *Daniel Boone,* calling *Meriwether Lewis.*" It was Rafe Barrot's voice.

Tom reached for the com. "Captain Barrot—"

"They took over the ship!" screamed Foster, at the top of his lungs. "I'm being held hostage by the robot!" The veins of his neck and temples bulged as he strained against Aristotle's hold.

"There's been a problem, Captain," said Tom. "I don't know how to explain it, but—"

"We received your report, Tom. Ben transmitted everything, including Lieutenant Foster's planned course. Under the circumstances, the lieutenant should consider himself under arrest. Whether you confine him to his quarters, or allow him to function as a crew member, is up to *you*, Tom. I am hereby transferring command of the *Meriwether Lewis* to you."

"But—wait—" Foster sputtered.

Rafe Barrot's voice crackled with anger over the speaker, "Don't make your situation any worse by disobeying orders, Lieutenant," he snapped. "Is the rest of your mission in jeopardy, Tom? Will you have to scrub it?"

"Negative, Captain," said Tom. "I'm lower on attitude engine fuel than I'd like to be, but we'll make it."

"Carry on, then, but keep me posted on your progress."

"Captain Barrot?"

"Yes, Tom?"

"We have a lot of . . . er . . . *unexpected* data on the atmosphere of Jupiter. The sensors and the exterior cameras were in operation the whole time. I'd like to transmit it so that the Friedmans can begin their analysis."

Rafe Barrot chuckled. "At least something worthwhile came from your unscheduled pass!

We're ready on this end, so transmit what you've got. And—good luck, Tom!"

Lieutenant Foster stormed off the bridge, his face white with anger, as Tom began setting their course for Io.

"It's down *there?*" Anita asked in disbelief. The young redhead floated just behind Tom's couch, using it to anchor herself in front of the glassite viewport. She and Tom watched, fascinated, as the *Meriwether Lewis* cruised slowly above the hostile-looking surface of Io.

Tom nodded. "This is our third orbit of Io at low altitude. The ship's sensors indicate that the Argus probe is inside the crater of that dead volcano ahead of us." Tom twisted around on his couch to face Ben Walking Eagle, who was bent over his computer terminal like an anxious mother hen. "When are the computer photographs from the first pass coming through?" he asked.

"Any minute," Ben replied, still intent on his work. "It takes a while to get hard copy from our setup."

"Art is a very fragile thing which cannot be rushed," said Aristotle, who was standing beside Ben, helping him with the computer. Tom smiled. He had the feeling that even though Aristotle was a machine, the robot was as anxious to see the photos as the humans were.

Tom suddenly realized that ever since they had begun their trip in the *Meriwether Lewis,* Aristotle had gradually become more like his old self. It was almost as if something on Io was erasing the robot's earlier moodiness.

He stared at the multicolored surface of the innermost Galilean moon of Jupiter with a mixture of curiosity and dread.

In some places, it was flat and marbled with streaks of fiery red, sulfurous yellow, and carbon black—like Yellowstone National Park without trees. Mostly, however, it was swollen and broken by the huge cones of volcanos, which rose like giant, infected sores from the tortured landscape. A few of the volcanos, such as the one toward which the ship was heading, appeared to be dead. Their sides were blackened by ancient layers of hardened magma and no fountains of liquid rock spurted from their mouths. The majority, however, were streaked by glowing streams of molten lava running down their sides, red-hot and deadly. Tom was extremely careful to steer the *Meriwether Lewis* around their gaping craters filled with boiling liquid rock.

"Wait'll you see what the cameras got!" Ben

suddenly exclaimed. "The pictures are coming through now and the computer really did a first-class job of putting them together!"

Anita floated over to where he and Aristotle were carefully taking the photos out of the computer's printer. "They're spectacular!" she agreed.

"Hey, you guys," said Tom from the pilot's couch, "stop oo-ing and ah-ing and let me see, too! I can't drop what I'm doing to come over there!"

Ben chuckled. "Sorry, buddy." He brought a small stack of the photos to Tom and pointed to a curiously indistinct object that gave off a metallic reflection. "I'm sure that's the Argus probe. This photo is from the first pass above the crater. It seems we went right over it, just as the sensors said we did."

"It surely doesn't look like the Argus probe the way I remember it! It's the wrong shape," Tom objected.

"The image could be distorted by the high radiation level," said Anita. "We were entering the flux tube."

The three young people and Aristotle watched as Jupiter became visible in the viewport from around the edge of Io. They had not known what

to expect when they first entered the area between the giant planet and Io, called the flux
tube by scientists. It was a region of mysteriously
high electromagnetic energy and intense radio
radiation. The only effect, however, had been a
sudden jump in the instrument readings.

There were various theories about the flux
tube's existence and its effects. The most promi-
nent one attributed the material composition of
Jupiter and Io as its source. What would it be like
to be on the surface of Io in this region? No one
knew.

Tom Swift and his crew would be the first to
find out!

"You might be right about the flux tube affecting these photos," said Tom, "but the shape of
this object still looks awfully odd to me."

Ahead of them, the huge black cone of the
dead volcano bulged up from the surface. Tom
headed the ship directly for its mouth.

"That volcano was sure an unfortunate choice
as a landing site for Argus," said Ben. "If it had
been active, you would have lost the probe for
sure."

"I think Argus was fooled somehow by the size
of the crater," said Tom. "But that's the chance
you take when you send an instrument package

someplace without a human along to observe things and make independent decisions. The package we're carrying will have a better chance, since we'll be placing it exactly where we want it. When we check out Argus, we'll plant it."

"We don't have to land inside the crater of the volcano, do we?" asked Anita anxiously.

"I'm afraid so," Tom replied, noting the apprehension in her voice. "If we don't, we'll have to do a lot of climbing and that would be even more dangerous. Our sensors indicate that the volcano is not active, so I don't think there is much risk if we don't linger too long."

"I believe Lieutenant Foster is coming onto the bridge, Tom," said Aristotle.

Tom felt a twinge of apprehension. Rafe Barrot had given him the choice of confining Foster to his quarters, or allowing him the freedom of the ship. Tom had taken the lieutenant's word of honor that he would cause no further trouble. But Foster had been very withdrawn since his "arrest" and had spent most of his time in his cabin, leaving Tom to run the ship. He seldom talked unless spoken to. Outwardly, he appeared calm, but Anita could not stand to be around him when she had her computer operating, so Tom knew that Foster was suppressing considerable emotion. Had he learned his lesson after the near-fatal encounter with Jupiter? Tom wanted to think so, but Anita, Ben, and even Aristotle did not agree.

Foster pulled himself onto the bridge by grasping the bulkhead handholds and paused uncertainly.

"We're getting ready to touch down on the surface," Tom said to him. "I could use your help up here." He indicated the now unoccupied copilot's couch.

Foster merely shrugged and pulled himself upon the couch without comment. It was a step in the right direction, anyway, Tom thought to himself.

"Assume positions for landing," Tom called and everyone strapped themselves in.

Finally, he cut the attitude engines and braced himself against the couch. Two seconds later, the *Meriwether Lewis*'s landing supports met the surface of Io with a bone-jarring thud. The ship bounced twice on its shock absorbers and then was still.

"Oh, man, do I ever feel *heavy!*" groaned Ben. He unsnapped his restraining harness and stood up with visible effort. Even though the gravity of Io was very close to that of Earth's Moon, the relatively long time in the weightless conditions of deep space had taken its toll on everyone's muscles.

Tom rose from his pilot's couch and stretched. This was going to take some getting used to, he thought ruefully.

"Tom—" Aristotle spoke up.

The young man turned, startled by the urgency in the robot's tone. The next moment, it appeared as if the deck of the *Meriwether Lewis* were being pulled out from under him and he fell to his knees. The entire ship began to shake violently.

"Moonquake!" yelled Foster.

Chapter Thirteen

"Everyone get down!" Tom ordered.

The instruments rattled in their housings and the very framework of the ship groaned with the force of the quake.

"I regret that I was unable to warn you sooner," Aristotle apologized. "My sensors picked up the quake only a moment before it happened. I suppose you could say that it crept up on me! Oh, how can you stand to have a flawed mechanism like me around?" he finished woefully.

The quake was over as suddenly as it had begun. Tom breathed a sigh of relief and got to his feet.

"I thought you said this volcano was inactive!" Foster shouted angrily.

"Ben?" Tom asked, concerned. "Is the volcano going to erupt?"

"The sensors don't indicate it," the young computer tech replied, "but I could be misinterpreting their data. I'm going to run tests of my own just to make sure!"

Tom could tell that Ben was upset about the surprise quake.

Could they be in danger, even as they discussed the situation?

"Io is volcanically active all over," said Anita. "I bet the quakes occur frequently and that they're normal. We'll just have to get used to them."

"If the instruments are to be trusted, you're right," said Tom. "Still—" He didn't finish the sentence. But the doubt had already been planted in everyone's mind.

"Ben, you stay here and work on the quake problem," said Tom. "Aristotle will help you. I'll take Anita and Lieutenant Foster with me. We'll make a short trip to the probe and plant the Friedmans' instrument package, then come back to the ship to run a few tests."

He motioned to Anita and the lieutenant.

"Let's suit up and take care of business so we can get out of here!"

"Good idea," said Anita.

Foster shrugged and said nothing.

As Tom popped the airlock hatch he instantly felt a mind-searing pain of high-pitched radio static. He gasped with shock, fumbled for the controls of his suit radio, and snapped it off.

Anita had fallen to her knees, clasping her hands against the plexiglass helmet in a useless reflex gesture against the pain. Foster had collapsed to the airlock floor and seemed to be unconscious.

Tom rushed over to Anita and shook her to get her attention, then motioned for her to turn off her suit radio. She reacted groggily, but a moment later, he could see the relief on her face.

Tom and Anita shook Foster hard and somehow managed to communicate the message to him. Still weak from the shock, the three young people watched the ladder tumble down from the hatch to the surface of Io.

They had to have their suit radios. Tom tried an experiment. He pulled his antenna in all the way, then thumbed the high-filter button on his helmet up to full. Then, carefully, he switched his suit radio back on with the volume at its lowest setting.

He winced as bursts of static assaulted his injured eardrum again; but this time, it was at a tolerable level. He motioned for Anita and Foster—who had opened his eyes—to do the same.

"What happened?" Anita asked. Tom could barely hear her through the static.

"The flux tube effect, I guess," he answered. "The radio radiation between Jupiter and Io is just too much for the suit radios. I'll have to make some modifications when we get back to the ship. Right now, I want to take a look at Argus. We can travel with our radios off, since Ben can break in and turn on the emergency band from the ship if he has to. Just stay in sight and tap your helmet twice at the base of your antenna if you want to communicate."

He turned and backed down the ladder carefully. It was slow going because his heavy boots made him clumsy and it was difficult to grip with his thick, shielded gloves. In addition, the instrument package strapped to his back kept pulling him slightly off center.

Unexpectedly, he felt an attack of vertigo and paused on the ladder in an effort to control the sickening nausea that accompanied it. It certainly would not be a good idea to throw up inside his space suit! The feeling alarmed him because in all the time he had been flying, he had never experienced vertigo, the sensation of sudden dizziness and loss of directional orientation.

Why now?

Tom looked up and instantly knew the answer. At the spot where he had paused on the ladder, he had cleared the ship. The striped face of Jupiter now occupied his vision, and it was bigger than anything he had ever seen. The hazy atmosphere of the gas giant dipped and moved before his eyes. From his position, he could see neither space nor Io—only the hypnotic swirls of Jupiter, a few hundred thousand miles away.

When Tom looked down at the surface of Io, he felt much better.

He jumped from the last rung of the ladder to the ground. It was only a short distance, but there was a stabbing pain in his knees from contact with the solid, lava-rock floor of the crater. He stepped to one side and steadied the ladder for Anita. She tapped her helmet twice.

"Where is Argus?" the redhead asked as she jumped down beside Tom.

"I didn't want to put the *Meriweather Lewis* too close to it," Tom replied. "The heat from our landing probably wouldn't have affected it, but I didn't want to take any chances of destroying any physical evidence of what's causing it to malfunction."

Anita nodded. "We're in for a hike then."

When Burt Foster was safely on the ground, the three young people set out to find the probe with an electronic locator Tom had attached to his suit's utility belt.

Ground that had appeared smooth from hundreds of feet above the moon was, close up, quite rugged. Looking around, Tom saw how Argus's sensors could easily have been fooled by the size and geological formations of the crater. Its vastness reminded him of the Great Salt Lake Valley in Utah—as it must have looked two million years ago, that is!

Tom moved uncomfortably in his suit. He could feel perspiration running down his back. It was difficult to get good footholds in the lava rock that had hardened in intricate and convoluted flow-patterns. Even in the one-sixth gravity of Io, the exertion of their hike was taking its toll on all of them, especially on Anita.

Although she kept herself in the best possible physical condition, having to manipulate her artificial leg under these conditions was very trying.

At this rate, they would use their breathing mixture in a very short time. Tom wished they could have taken a rover, but he knew the terrain of Io would have been far too hazardous for any of the machines the expedition had brought. Machines were wonderfully convenient, at times, but they were restrictive and less adaptable than man.

The young inventor checked the locator on his belt. The tiny light in the center of it pulsed strongly. That meant they were getting close. Ahead of them was a steep lava hill that they would have to climb or go around. Tom signaled a halt and indicated that Foster and Anita should turn on their suit radios.

"Ten minutes rest stop," he said through the maddening static.

"I can use it," he heard Anita say, and watched as she checked the ground for sharp stones that could puncture her suit before sinking down gratefully.

Foster, still stubborn and defiant, chose to stand. "We're wasting ten minutes of air," he argued. "If Ms. Thorwald can't stand the pace, she should go back to the ship!"

"Take ten minutes, Lieutenant," said Tom. "That's an order. I don't care how you use it, but I'd advise you to sit down and rest while I decide where we should go from here!"

Foster made an obvious show of switching off

his suit and then, to Tom's surprise, began to climb the hill, not looking back.

It was the first order Burt Foster had openly disobeyed. Would Tom have to use force to control the lieutenant? He hoped not.

"Ship to shore party!" Ben's urgent voice broke through their radios on the emergency band. "Mayday! Mayday! Brace yourselves for another moonquake! Aristotle says—"

Tom did not wait for him to finish, but flattened himself onto the rocky surface. Anita did the same. Both looked in the direction that Foster had gone and saw him on the hill above them.

He was ignoring Ben's warning.

Tom felt a vibration coming from deep inside the surface and tensed his muscles for the coming shock.

It was as though Io was having a violent convulsion.

Anita screamed as bits of rock began to pelt their suits, rolling down from above.

Tom looked up to see Burt Foster sliding down the hill toward them, very fast and totally out of control.

One tiny hole in his spacesuit and the man's blood would quickly freeze in the chill vacuum of space!

"We've got to catch him!" Tom shouted to Anita.

"I'll do my best!" she cried.

Foster was trying to grab a handhold on the rock, but he was moving too fast. Tom winced as small stones pelted him, broken off by the lieutenant's desperate effort to stop his fall.

"Brace yourself, Anita," he called out. "We'll have to use our bodies to break his momentum!"

"I always loved tackle football," was her answer.

"Here he comes," shouted Tom. "Grab him!"

They reached for Foster's suit while trying to keep from being dragged down with him.

But they could not hold him.

Anita let go first, and clawed desperately at the shaking surface of the crater.

"I'm sorry," she wailed.

Foster's weight was too much for Tom. He felt helpless as the lieutenant slid by him.

Tom whipped his body around to try to catch the man from behind and a sickening feeling of fear stabbed him as the smooth fabric of Foster's spacesuit slipped through his gloved hands.

Then he froze in terror!

The moonquake had cracked open the surface. A yawning chasm, of a size that could swallow them all and take the *Meriwether Lewis* with them, gaped just below where he and Anita were desperately clinging. Foster would slide right into it if he couldn't stop himself!

Chapter Fourteen

Tom tried to get up, but he couldn't keep his balance. The heaving surface threw him back down again.

Hard.

He watched Foster, helplessly.

The young lieutenant's legs went over the side of the split and Tom saw him make a last desperate attempt to grab the lava rock.

Foster's grip held! His legs dangled into the huge rip of the crater, but as long as he could hold on, he would not fall in.

Then Tom felt a lessening in the quake's intensity. He hoped it would be enough to allow him to reach Foster.

"I'll try and get him," he said to Anita.

"I'm going with you!" she responded.

"No, you'll get hurt."

"Tom, you might need my help," she called out.

Tom had to admit she was right. "Okay, follow me," he agreed.

They were able to stand and keep their balance, even though the surface under them trembled. They reached the young officer quickly. It was a simple matter to pull him off the edge of the chasm. Tom chanced a look down and gulped when he couldn't see the bottom that was hidden in the depths of darkness.

As soon as he was on his feet, Foster struggled to break free of Tom and Anita. Instead of being grateful, Tom realized with a shock, the young lieutenant was angry!

Foster switched on his suit radio. "Why did you two change your minds?" he asked. "You let me fall, hoping I'd get killed so you could invent some kind of coverup story for Captain Barrot. But you lost your nerve at the last minute!"

"That's a lie!" Tom shouted into his radio. "You disobeyed orders by going up that hill alone and then you completely ignored the warning from the ship. We tried to catch you when you fell and you know it!"

Anita looked at the darkly handsome officer through his helmet faceplate. "You're really twisted, Foster!" she said contemptuously.

"Ship to shore party," Ben cut in, anxiously. "Come in! What's going on out there?"

"It's nothing serious," Tom replied. "Just a little disagreement. Thanks for the warning about the quake. I think it saved our lives."

"You can thank Aristotle for that," said Ben. "I was busy waiting for the rest of the computer composite photos when he gave the warning. Are you guys coming back now?"

"I want to retrieve the probe and plant the instruments, Ben," said Tom. He looked questioningly at Anita.

"I'm going, too," she said.

"Foster?"

"I wouldn't miss a chance to see the great Tom Swift swallowed by the volcano!" replied the young lieutenant.

"I'm keeping all channels open from now on," Ben told them. "I'll try and fight the static by boosting signals from the ship's computer. That might help. The minute I get any more warnings, I'll holler."

Tom turned and started back up the hill, followed by the others.

A few minutes later they reached the top of the

lava-rock mound and stared in amazement into the valley below them!

In the center of it stood the Argus probe, and next to it—or rather, almost on top of it—hovered the strangest craft Tom had ever seen. It looked like a huge metal insect and it loomed over the probe as though that machine were its prey.

"Wh-what is it?" breathed Anita.

"It doesn't appear to be one of ours," Foster declared. He seemed to have momentarily forgotten his personal hatred for Tom and Anita. "I would know if our military had that kind of design in the works."

"What's going on?" Ben broke in. "What have you found?"

"Argus has company," answered Tom. "You'd better send Aristotle down here right away. I'm going to need him."

"I am on the way," came the robot's instant reply.

"Swift Enterprises hasn't anything even remotely resembling that thing," Tom continued, thoughtfully. "How about the Luna Corporation? Could this be one of their long-range exploratory probes?"

Anita snorted in disgust at the mention of the Swifts' multinational competitor. It rivaled Swift

Enterprises in size and daring, but lacked its impeccable reputation.

"If nobody has a design like that for a probe—even on the drawing board—then the Luna Corporation couldn't possibly have sent it up here." She snorted again. "There wouldn't have been anything for the great David Luna to *steal!*"

Tom had to admit that the probe had a unique design. It consisted of three distinct parts. The head, shaped like an inverted teardrop, contained two huge multifaceted lenses and what appeared to be the same sort of sensing equipment that Aristotle had in his sensorframe. The head terminated in two powerful-looking metal pincers or mechanical hands, hydraulically operated.

The head was connected to the frame of the probe's exo-skeleton. What Tom knew had to be the "brain" of the probe was housed in the center of the exo-skeleton. It was a smooth, egg-shaped object with a sculptured handle molded into it. The handle was obviously for installation and removal purposes.

Tom could see that it was built for a hand much like his own!

The probe's "legs" extended down from the mainframe. There were eight of them and they were jointed in several places. Again, there was evidence of hydraulic operation. That meant that the probe could actually walk—when it had all of its pod-like "feet." Two of these seemed to be missing and two more looked twisted into unnatural positions. It was hard to tell from a distance.

"It could be an alien probe," Tom said finally.

"That's ridiculous!" Foster sneered. "The navy has done studies on the possibilities of life in outer space and the odds are strictly *against* another life form like ours existing anywhere in the galaxy!"

"Why does it have to be a humanoid life form?" Tom asked. "A one-celled amoeba, an elephant, and a dandelion are also life forms. So's a palm tree and a boa constrictor. The possibilities are endless, even on Earth. Just think how many different variations there are of human beings alone. When was the last time you saw even two people who were exactly alike?"

"*That's* for sure," commented Anita.

"You're crazy, Swift," argued Foster. "None of those other life forms are capable of building and launching a space probe. They're all vastly inferior to us."

"That still doesn't prove anything, in my opinion," said Anita, "and I'm basing my statement on the fact that that thing down there is staring at us!"

As if to confirm Anita's point, the strange probe cocked its head to one side, seemingly questioning the behavior of the alien beings observing it. The action reminded Tom of a praying mantis he had once seen in his garden at home. He had spent an hour watching it watch him and wondering what thoughts were passing through that insectile brain.

"You're right, Anita!" he exclaimed. "It knows we're here. It's 'aware'!"

"That makes it more of a robot than an actual probe as we apply the term," said Ben who had been listening intently over the radio. "It may be intelligent. I'd be careful."

"I'm going down there and have a closer look at it," said Tom.

"This is a top-secret discovery," Foster declared. There was a tone in his voice that Tom did not like. It had a hint of trouble in it. "I'm going with you as a representative of the United States Government."

"Why don't you admit that you're afraid we'll find something and take credit for it, leaving you out in the cold? That's it, isn't it?" Anita burst out angrily.

Foster glowered at her, but did not pursue the argument.

Quickly, but carefully, the three young people picked their way down the lava-rock slope, their eyes on the probe. Its glittering, multifaceted eyes watched them.

At the base of the slope, the ground leveled out. Tom, Anita, and Foster edged toward the probe slowly and deliberately from that point on. They did not want any of their actions to be interpreted as hostile.

When they were a hundred yards away, Tom called a halt. The young, six-foot-tall inventor was now able to judge the probe's size more accurately. It stood just about seven inches taller than he was.

"The probe's legs are stuck in the rock!" exclaimed Foster. "The thing must have landed here when the volcano was still active and the lava solidified around it, trapping it!"

"The broken legs may be from its efforts to free itself," said Tom. "I wonder why Argus landed so close to it. Ben, I'm going to signal Argus to start transmitting data. If the cameras are still operative, the pictures might tell us something. Are you and the computer standing by to collect what it sends?"

"I'm set up now," Ben replied from the ship,

"but the pictures from the second Io pass, over this volcano, are being assembled, so is it okay if I put the Argus data on hold for a while? I'm still trying to find out if we can expect an eruption any time soon!"

"Sure," said Tom. "Stand by." He pressed a button on the locator he had used to track the probe. It sent an invisible light-beam radio signal to the squat mechanoid. The hundred eyes of Argus—its sensors—began to glow in recognition.

Instantly, two ruby-red beams shot from the eyes of the insect probe and converged inches away from Tom's boots. Tom jumped back, alarmed. The beams had burned into the lava rock as though it were ice cream.

"It picked up my signal to Argus and it's warning me to keep my distance," said Tom. The young inventor knew that if the probe had wanted to kill him, he would now be quite dead. He shuddered involuntarily.

But why did the alien want him to stay away from Argus?

"The probe's signal is being blocked, Tom," said Ben.

"I know," said Tom, worriedly. "The alien seems to be holding it hostage."

"What?" asked the young computer tech. "Why—"

The rest of Ben's sentence was drowned out by a high-pitched screeching noise.

Suddenly, a bolt of visible energy shot from the surface of Jupiter like lightning and struck the crater's surface. A shower of rock exploded into space, only a few miles away.

The head of the alien probe swiveled around to follow the strange lightning.

The effect was over in seconds.

"What happened?" yelled Foster. Tom could tell the lieutenant was afraid. He had good reason to be. The bolt of lightning could easily have struck them!

"It's part of the flux tube effect," said Tom. "For unknown reasons, those exchanges of visible energy happen frequently here. It may have to do with the cores of Jupiter and Io reacting to each other."

"It sure caused a lot of radio interference," said Ben.

"Look out!" Anita suddenly screamed. "The alien is going to shoot at us!"

Chapter Fifteen

The probe's eyes glowed angrily, and Tom knew they could not possibly outrun its beams. But why was it going to shoot at them?

Abruptly, the destructive light in the probe's eyes died and it seemed to look past them. Tom whirled around to see Aristotle coming toward the group.

"It was just a misunderstanding, Tom," the robot said. "The alien thought you were trying to trick it. A similar energy phenomenon brought it here in search of intelligent life. When it arrived, it realized it had made a mistake and there was no life here, but not before it became trapped. I am glad that I intervened in time."

173

"You communicated with it?" asked Tom, flabbergasted.

"Yes. The alien has analyzed the programing of Argus and can communicate in binary."

"Has it come to destroy Earth?" Foster asked, his voice shaking slightly.

"You've been watching too many science fiction movies, Lieutenant," commented Ben over the radio. "I'm glad you got there in time to prevent an accident, Aristotle."

"I am relieved that the alien did not destroy my creator," replied the robot.

"Why did you call it 'the alien,' Aristotle?" asked Tom.

"The probe is from the Alpha Centauri system. I think that qualifies it as alien," replied the mechanoid.

"That's right here in our own galaxy!" Anita exclaimed. "I always thought that if we had visitors from outer space, they'd be from another galaxy—like Andromeda, for example."

"On the contrary," said Tom. "Think of the distances you're talking about when you use the term 'our galaxy.' Our Sun is just one dinky star in the whole Milky Way galaxy. Alpha Centauri is another dinky star. Sure, it happens to be our closest neighbor, but it's still over one parsec from us—over three light years. If we could travel at the speed of light, we could make it in about four years."

Anita nodded.

"The Andromeda galaxy, on the other hand, is two million, two hundred thousand light years away," broke in Ben. "Any civilization that sent out a probe from there would probably be dead by the time it got even halfway to us—even traveling at light speed!"

"Right," Tom said. "We can now go at one-tenth the speed of light with our present technology fusion drive. At that rate, it would take us about four hundred years to get to the people who sent this probe!"

"You mean it traveled four hundred years to get here?" asked Anita.

Tom turned to Aristotle questioningly. "*Has* it? And how long has it been stuck on Io?"

Aristotle was silent a moment. When he spoke, the robot sounded flustered.

"No, Tom. The alien has not been . . . traveling . . . for that length of time. It will not tell me how long its journey was from its exact point of origin. However, it had been *here* a much longer time. One revolution of the striped gas giant—Jupiter—around its primary."

"That's twelve Earth years!" Tom exclaimed. "If it has been stuck on Io longer than the time it took getting here, the alien's civilization must have some kind of star drive!"

"That is correct," continued Aristotle. "The alien is a messenger, but it will not divulge its message until the proper time. I do not understand its motives or purpose, but the message is of such importance that we must be deemed worthy to receive it. What criterion the alien will use to make this determination, I also do not know. It is an impatient and short-tempered mechanism, Tom. That is due to its long entrapment and the urgency of its message. I am sorry I have failed to find out the specific information you asked for."

"You haven't failed, Aristotle," said Tom. "After all, you are the only one who can talk to the alien. Is it difficult for you to talk to it?"

"Yes, Tom. However, I am also relieved by finding this presence."

"Relieved?" asked Anita.

"Yes, circuit brother. Shortly after the *Daniel Boone* began its present journey, I became aware of some extremely low-frequency impulses. They were obviously of more than random nature but not from any human source."

"Is that why you were so quiet when we were in orbit around Ganymede?" Tom asked.

"Exactly. I was troubled because the nature of

the impulses, as well as their source, was constantly eluding me. However, as we drew closer to Io, it became obvious the source of the mysterious impulses was this moon."

"Aristotle," Anita laughed. "You are something of an empath yourself!"

"Tom!" Ben's voice came over the radio.

"What is it, Ben?"

"I've just finished scanning the computer photos and we could be in serious trouble!"

"The volcano?" asked Anita worriedly.

"Yep. I analyzed the pictures from our second pass and everything looked normal. Then I compared them with the ones from the first pass. There's a bulge that's growing bigger by the hour on the north side of the cone. This means we have a lot of pressure build-up under the surface. The frequency of the moonquakes is also an indication of that. I think the volcano is about to blow!"

"Oh, no! We've just made what might be the scientific discovery of all time and now we're about to lose it!" Tom cried out, frustrated.

Foster turned to Aristotle. "Tell the probe that I'm a representative of the United States Government and that I'm authorized to receive any message the alien might have. I am a navy officer, you know!"

Before Tom or Anita could protest, Ben's voice broke in again. "I think you all better get back to the ship!" he urged.

"I've got to rescue Argus," said Tom.

"Argus can be of no further use to you, Tom," Aristotle declared. "Its mind is gone." There was a note of sadness in the robot's voice. "Exposure to the probing of the alien was too much for its simple circuits."

"We could take the alien with us, but it won't let us near it," said Tom. "Can't you find out its message?"

Suddenly the ground beneath them began to shake.

"We have to go!" pleaded Anita.

The alien probe swayed on its spidery legs for a moment and was still.

"It was only a harmonic tremor," said Tom, relieved. "But another moonquake is sure to follow."

"The alien informs me that the events taking place resemble those that brought about its entrapment!" said Aristotle.

"I don't like this situation," Ben declared tensely.

"Aristotle, inform the alien that we want to take it with us," said Tom, "and that if it doesn't wish to go, it must tell us the message now because we're leaving."

"The alien is not responding," said Aristotle.

"My air-level indicator just changed over, Tom," Anita said tensely. "I've only got a few more minutes of air left."

Suddenly, another flash of energy shot from Jupiter to Io. An explosion of rock marked its landing.

"Io *must* be some kind of ground for electrical energy generated in the atmosphere of Jupiter at certain times in its revolution," Tom commented.

"And it must trigger the volcano every twelve years," said Foster. "We can't leave the probe here, Tom! If we could analyze its star drive, we'd have the secret of interstellar travel! We could build the mightiest army in the galaxy! Don't you understand what that would mean?"

"I understand that if we don't get out of here, we're all going to be fried!" said Tom. "Let's go!"

"Look at the alien probe!" yelled Anita. "It's moving!"

The young people watched as the strange instrument applied all its hydraulic force to the trapped legs.

"Get back!" Tom shouted. "It's trying to break free of the lava rock."

"It won't work!" cried Anita, dismayed.

The ground under them began to tremble.

"Get out of there!" Ben commanded over the radio. "The entire crater is beginning to break up!"

"The volcano is erupting?" asked Foster, panic-stricken.

"It looks that way," said Tom. "If we don't leave now, we'll get trapped like the alien—or worse! Head for the ship, everybody."

Foster cast a mournful glance at the alien probe, then he and Anita began running for the *Meriwether Lewis*.

"Come on, Aristotle," said Tom.

"Wait!" cried the robot. "The alien is a messenger from beings who call themselves the Skree. It has come in search of help against something it calls the Chutans—beings who are conducting a war of conquest against the Skree."

"Come on, Aristotle. There's no time left!" said Tom.

"No! It must not fail in its mission. The alien captured Argus, reasoning that the beings who constructed that mechanoid would come for it. You came. The alien wishes to go with us."

"I can't pull it out of the lava now," said Tom. "There's just no time!"

"The alien knows it cannot remain whole and fulfill its mission. It wants you to remove the memory core, Tom. It offers the secret of the star drive in exchange."

Tom was torn between the risk of survival and his scientific instincts. The alien made the choice simpler. As Tom and Aristotle watched, fascinated, it unlocked its egg-shaped brain core from its exo-skeleton.

"Unplug the sensor cables, Tom," urged Aristotle. "Hurry."

Tom threw caution aside and rapidly approached the alien probe. It made no move to stop him. Reaching up, he disconnected all the cables he could see between the probe and the exo-skeleton. One by one, its systems seemed to die.

Could a machine die? Tom wondered.

It was truly as if the life force of the probe had suddenly gone out. Without the brain core, the strange craft was only a lifeless piece of hardware.

Tom lifted the core out of the exo-skeleton and cradled it in his arms.

"Head for the ship!" he shouted to Aristotle.

As they raced for the shelter of the *Meriwether Lewis,* Tom felt the weight of the instrument package strapped to his back. In the excitement of the discovery of another life form, he had completely forgotten about planting the package!

Where could he place it so it would survive the quake? Even if it was damaged by the natural forces on this volcanic moon, the information it would gather would go a long way toward explaining the flux tube to scientists. He *had* to take just one more moment and fulfill his original mission!

"Aristotle!" he called to his robot. "Remove the package on my back, please! Hurry!"

As the robot deftly unfastened the straps, the ground began to buck and sway even more ferociously.

"Tom!" Ben shouted anxiously. "Forget it! You life is more important!"

"Coming, Ben. Prepare to lift off the instant we are aboard," Tom replied as he felt the weight being taken from his back.

Aristotle placed the instrument pack on the broad, relatively flat surface of an enormous slab of lava rock.

"That is the best we can do without more time for studies," Aristotle said sadly.

"Okay," Tom said as they began to run for the

ship. "It is still better than not having placed it at all."

Seconds later, Tom burst through the hatch onto the bridge of the *Meriwether Lewis.* He had removed his helmet, but there was no time to take off his suit. He leaped onto the pilot's couch and yanked the crash harness into place. Ben, Anita, and Burt Foster were already strapped in, waiting anxiously. Aristotle had attached himself to the deck of the ship with his powerful electro-magnetic motorframe and was cradling the alien probe's brain core carefully.

"Get ready," shouted Tom. "I'm giving the fusion drive its head! If I don't we'll be cooked!"

They felt the ground heaving under the ship as he coaxed the powerful fusion drive into life.

It woke with a roar and the *Meriwether Lewis* climbed rapidly into the black void of space.

"I—I can't breathe!" croaked Foster.

"This is the *Daniel Boone* calling!" Rafe Barrot's voice sounded anxious. "We just picked you up on the screen and you're traveling like a bullet!"

Tom gently eased back on the power. He welcomed the sudden release of pressure, and the others gasped with relief.

"Daniel Boone," said Tom. "We're really glad to hear from you!"

"What happened? We lost you when you entered the flux tube. Did you find Argus? Its signal died a while ago."

"Argus was destroyed in the eruption of a volcano on Io, Captain. We barely escaped ourselves.

"The instrument package was placed and activated. Tell the Friedmans we are monitoring and storing its signals."

Tom wanted to tell Rafe Barrot all about finding the alien probe and about the Skree and the star drive, but he knew that Burt Foster had been right about one thing. It was a top-secret find and if the information fell into the wrong hands, it could have untold consequences for the planet Earth. He sighed wearily. "We're coming in, Captain. Have my father and a top-security team standing by to meet us at the hanger deck. I'll make a full report at that time."

There was a slight pause, then Rafe Barrot said, "Will do, Tom. A top-security team is assembling now. Welcome back."

Yes, it would be some welcome. He stretched back on his pilot's couch and thought about what the rest of the alien's message might be. He smiled to himself. Maybe Foster hadn't been watching too many science-fiction movies after all.

Tom suspected he would have his greatest adventure yet finding out. But little did he realize what incredible events were in store for him in *Tom Swift: The Alien Probe.*

THE TOM SWIFT ® SERIES
by Victor Appleton

The City in the Stars (#1)
Terror on the Moons of Jupiter (#2)
The Alien Probe (#3)
The War in Outer Space (#4)
The Astral Fortress (#5)
The Rescue Mission (#6)
Ark Two (#7)
The Crater of Mystery (#8)

You will also enjoy

THE HARDY BOYS ® SERIES
by Franklin W. Dixon

Night of the Werewolf (#59)
Mystery of the Samurai Sword (#60)
The Pentagon Spy (#61)
The Apeman's Secret (#62)
The Mummy Case (#63)
Mystery of Smugglers Cove (#64)
The Stone Idol (#65)
The Vanishing Thieves (#66)
The Outlaw's Silver (#67)
The Submarine Caper (#68)
The Four-Headed Dragon (#69)
The Infinity Clue (#70)
Track of the Zombie (#71)
The Voodoo Plot (#72)
The Billion Dollar Ransom (#73)
Tic-Tac-Terror (#74)
Trapped at Sea (#75)
Game Plan for Disaster (#76)